I0788118

Fae Captive

Tangled Fae: Book Two

Sarah K. L. Wilson

Published by Sarah K. L. Wilson, 2020.

This is a work of fiction. Similarities to real people, places, or events are entirely coincidental.

FAE CAPTIVE

First edition. February 13, 2020.

Copyright © 2020 Sarah K. L. Wilson.

Written by Sarah K. L. Wilson.

For Cale, always.

Other Books by Sarah K. L. Wilson

Dragon School Series
First Flight
Initiate
The Dark Prince
The Ruby Isles
Sworn
Dusk Covenant
First Message
Warring Promises
Prince of Dragons
Dark Night
Bright Hopes
Mark of Loyalty
Dire Quest
Ancient Allies
Pipe of Wings
Dragon Piper
Dust of Death
Troubled War
Starie Night
Ascendant Light
Dragon Chameleon Series
Rogue's Quest
Paths of Deception
City of Ice
Mist of Power
Silver Eyes
World of Legends
Chase the Moon
Shadow Quest

Creeping Darkness
Golem Siege
Memory of Mountains
Color of Victory
Dragon Tide Series
Dragonlet
Dragon Staff
Desperate Flight
Bubbles of Hope
Waves of Destiny
Tides of Change
Keys of Power
Rock Eaters
Underworld
Chosen One
The Unweaving Chronicles Series
Teeth of the Gods
Lightning Strikes Twice
Thunder Rattles High
Bridge of Legends Series
Summernight
Dawnspell
Autumngale
Winterfast
Springhatch

BOOK ONE

*A wreath of writhing wraiths they were and wrath they had
a'plenty,
A twisted tawdry tangle they and called themselves the Gen-
try.
But lo, so beauteous to the eye, they did deceive the many,
And tied them up in webs of lies and sold them for a penny.
So, if you see a tangled Fae and think him sweet and bonny,
Think if you like your pretty head or coin so bright and
tawny.*
-Tales of the Faewald

Chapter One

My father. They'd nailed him to a tree. He was there in agony.

I wanted the shivering pain of that to fuel me, to feed the fire in me, to give me the strength to fight the fear of being shrunken down to the size of a hand and imprisoned. But the flame inside me was guttering. Every moment sent it shimmering a little further away.

"I should say something dramatic," Scouvrel said over the steady beat of the unicorn's hooves galloping on soft turf. "Something like, 'And so the Hunter has become the hunted.' But that just doesn't seem cruel enough for these circumstances.'"

"I should say something like, 'Rats always get out of the trap if you don't kill them right away' and give you a significant look so you know I mean you, but I'm afraid that might be an insult to rats," I shot back.

It had been all I could do, as we rode away from the smoke waterfall, to cling to the bars of the cage and try not to vomit again. The cage rocked wildly as the unicorn galloped across the turf of the Faewald. It didn't give me a chance to even take off my pack. The one time I'd let go of the bars, I'd slid across the cage floor and smashed into the bars on the other side. Now, I clung to them with both hands, trying to breathe evenly and remind myself that I didn't need to panic. Life wasn't over. I was just trapped.

Trapped animals sometimes got away. Of course, sometimes they had to chew off their own foot to do it. I could do that if I had to. I just had to find my fire again.

I reached for my blindfold. I wanted to see more than just the spirit world here. My second sight was far clearer, far more detailed than the spirit world at home. In fact, if I didn't know better, I would think I had my real sight back. I could easily see the purple glow around the white unicorn and the sparkling stars kicking up in its wake. But the colors were sharper, the lights brighter and the dark blacker. It was as if my second sight could see more here. As if I were in another world – which I was. Fancy that.

Would I be blind if I pulled the blindfold up now?

"Don't do it," Scouvrel warned, his tone mocking. "You'll regret it the moment you do. Truth will destroy you if you don't have a way to handle it."

"You say that," I said between gritted teeth as my stomach lurched again. I stood up, riding the rolling of the cage on my feet. "But I think you just want to hide your world from me and keep me helpless."

"Oh, it's so much worse than anything you're imagining," he said. "But who knows, maybe you'll like hell, you little nightmare."

"You say that like you think you're better than me. Like you can handle things I can't."

"Faeries are higher in the food chain, that's just a fact. We could eat mortals for breakfast, and I mean that quite literally. There are some of my kind who would consider that no different than venison," he said lightly. But he was distracted, as if he were searching for something from the back of the unicorn.

He thought he was somehow better than us? Better than me? A species apart? Why? Because he had magic and tricks? He'd better watch out. I would best him in every way. I would rub his nose in the fact that I am superior to anything his kind could ever dream of being. I would make all his magic look like sparks popping from a fire and make his trickery look like nothing but tatters.

I would. Even if I looked weak and pathetic in this cage right now.

"Make a bargain with me, Little Hunter," Scouvrel whispered, holding up my cage to stare inside. His dark eyes held a deep emotion I didn't understand.

I swallowed. He was *my* captor now. What was he going to do with all that power?

"What kind of a bargain? Can you free my father?"

"Not yet."

"Will you free me?"

"Not yet."

I narrowed my eyes. "Then no bargain."

"Reconsider," he cooed to me as if I could be swayed by his pretty words and curving sensuous lips. "If you will wait to pull up your blindfold until after we leave the stag, I will tell you why all of the Faewald wants to possess you now."

"They want *me*?"

"But of course." His smile was smooth and cool. He really was terrifyingly beautiful and the haunting purples and plums of the rolling moonlit hills behind him only made him more gorgeous.

Why would anyone in the Faewald want me – except as a way to get out. I frowned.

"It's a bargain," I agreed.

"It's a bargain." He seemed very pleased with himself. "Now ... the stag."

He turned the unicorn off the road and between the trees with a rough tug on its mane. It screamed a horsey scream at him and its feet tore up clumps of dirt.

"I don't think he likes you," I said grimly.

"He's not of my court. He's your sister's plaything. But he will serve his purpose before I return him."

Our journey reminded me almost of threading through the trees with my father as we set our traps. Even at this speed, I could see the little trails in the grass that ran across the path – evidence of rabbits. Larger trails with good deer sign. A rub on one of the trees. An old scrape. There was game here and plenty of it. Without thinking, I began to whistle my father's favorite tune.

Scouvrel froze.

So did the unicorn.

After a moment, I realized everything had frozen from the birds in the trees to the insects buzzing between the leaves and in the long grass. My whistle faded in the growing breeze.

"No music," I sighed. "Can you truly not make music, you glorious above-me Fae?"

Music was one power I had that Scouvrel didn't. But what did freezing them matter if I couldn't get out of the cage?

Scouvrel cleared his throat.

"We can't make beautiful sounds. Only true sounds. And you don't want to hear our hearts. Our hearts sing the everlasting scream of nothing."

I shivered.

"Ah, here's the stag."

I followed his eyes to where the trees parted, and a great hill rose up between craggy boulders and creaking oaks. In the center of the hill, a glowing bluish-white stag snorted and puffed, his breath hanging in the air even though it wasn't cold. He lowered his majestic head and waited as we climbed up the hill and stopped beside him. His antlers were blue lightning, ever flashing and bursting again.

With my spirit-sight he was three times the height of the unicorn and twice as thick, but he was also a glowing, transparent spirit of the forest. What creature could be more amazing than this? He could fling us aside with a single swipe of that lightning-rack. He could eviscerate us in a moment. I felt my hands trembling with excitement. I'd never been this close to a creature like this before. My father would –

My thought broke off abruptly.

The stag ignored us, his eyes fixed to the horizon, far beyond.

"It's time for me to take you into my confidence," Scouvrel said warily. He kept looking at me – like a boy who wanted me to join him in a prank – as he tied the unicorn to a poplar sapling with the slender branches of the sapling. It tried to bite his hand and he punched it in the nose. He hardly seemed to notice it, as if he punched unicorns every day.

"Why doesn't it just stab you and get it over with?" I asked.

"There's a head tax for killing me, too," Scouvrel said lightly as he held my cage up in the glow of the white crescent moon. "But back to what I want to talk about – the Faewald needs you, Little Hunter."

"The Faewald needs a Hunter?" I asked, crossing my arms.

"No – it needs the Oolag. The one connected to the land. We knew that one of you was the one. That's why Cavariel came for Hulanna," he said with a glimmer in his eye. "But he stole the wrong twin."

"So why pick *her* then?"

A figure emerged from behind the stomping stag. It was white and bright as the moon, a rack of antlers like a buck's protruded from her head. She wore a long, sweeping dress and a mask of silver fish scales that hid her face. Her voice creaked like a tree in high winds.

"Is it so ridiculous that we all assumed the prettier twin was the one blest by fate?" She was looking right at me.

"It's very Fae of you," I said dryly to her. "So, they want me because they chose the wrong sister. And here you've been telling me how Fae are better than mortals. Think again."

"Sooth," Scouvrel acknowledged. "You found us."

"I always find what I'm looking for. They found you for the prophecy, girl. And I'm here to speak it over you:

One born on a single day in two halves.
One half for the land. One for the air.
One for the rending. One for repair.

May the winds accept my words spoken over you."

She walked past me as if there was nothing more to say.

"She just shows up like that out of nowhere?" I protested.

"She's done saying your sooth. Why would she stay? You don't amuse her like you amuse me," Scouvrel said with a shrug. "She's always with the stag. He's the sign of portents and mysteries." Above us, the sign of portents huffed out a long breath and ducked his crowned head. "I brought you to her to hear for yourself. And now you've heard. The Courts want you because they chose the right twin in many ways, and yet she still wasn't enough. They want you to be the second half of what they need. And they'll do anything to get you."

I cleared my throat. And what could I do about any of that from inside this cage?

"And my sister? What does she want?"

"The Faewald," Scouvrel said grimly. "Now, isn't that nice? Which is why I need to teach you what is happening in this world before it swallows you up, Little Hunter."

There was a gleam of mistrust in his eyes. He shifted and the stag behind him disappeared in a crack of thunder as he held the cage up high and glared through the bars at me.

"You may not consider me a friend, but if you want your father free and your sister's mad gamble for power stopped, then I am your ally. And if I'm going to help you, I need to teach you my world as quickly as possible. I'll make a game of it if you think that will help."

I snorted at the twinkle in his eye. "Let me guess, the game is called 'Survival.'"

"An apt description."

Around us, the forest began to stir.

"They will send hunters after us. Smooth assassins bent on stealing us from the shadows," he warned, though his playful wink made it seem like a game. "Fortunately, you are guarded by iron bars."

"Yes, it's amazing I'm not more grateful."

He snorted. "Are you ready to learn everything you need to know about the Faewald?"

"Only if you start by answering one question," I said.

"Ask away, Little Nightmare."

"Why are we just standing in one place if they're hunting us?"

He laughed and leapt onto the unicorn, wrenching the poplar sapling aside and leaning low and aggressively over the saddle as if he could conquer the whole world from the back of a unicorn. Maybe he could. Maybe we were about to do that together.

Chapter Two

"The first thing you need to know," Scouvrel said, "Is that the Faewald is a place of constant change – constant shifting. What is here today is gone tomorrow."

I yawned dramatically. "And here you've been playing at being immortal."

"Pay attention, Little Nightmare," he said, leveling his gaze at me and gritting his teeth in a way that suggested violence and seduction all at once. "Without this knowledge, you're a goat ready to be gutted."

I remembered what the Fae had done to my goats. I felt my face freeze. He nodded as if he were reliving the same memory.

"Are there good and bad Fae?" I asked. We were back on the road now and it ran along a narrow ridge at the top of a hill that was barely wide enough for a horse track. Trees dotted the sides of the path, but the ground fell sharply away on either side, giving me a view of the starlit Faewald in every direction. I gasped as I saw a flashing satin sea in one direction and the spindly turrets of a sprawling castle in the other direction. The scents of the forest washed around us, bathing us in otherworldly savory sweetness – pine and thyme, soft meadows and something achingly sweet I couldn't identify.

My breath caught in my throat at how the moonlight picked out the details, for all the world like the Faewald of whispered stories and bedtime tales. I was here – inside a story. A terrible one, but still a story.

"Seelie and Unseelie?" Scouvrel's laugh was nasty. "That's a startale, Little Nightmare, and it's adorable that you've heard of it, but no. There are only bad and worse Fae. We bear no interest in altruism."

"What about fated mates? High Lord Cavariel – or whatever his name is – told Hulanna she was his fated mate."

"I never tire of your idealism," he said dryly. The unicorn paused, rearing up and pawing the air. Scouvrel seized it by the horn and shook it roughly until it calmed. That would never have worked with a real horse. He snarled at it, "Calm yourself, dead creature, or I will calm you and pay the head price with gladness."

His menacing voice even spooked me. It didn't help that he still had his hand wrapped in the eye of the brass needle like it was the grip of a sword. It was deadly sharp. His other hand clutched my cage.

"So fated mates are not a real thing?" I pressed.

"That's what we tell our victims as we drag them, drowning, into the depths of our depravity. 'Ah, but we are fated,' we say. 'Can't you feel the tether between us? Oh, it feels like a noose? Ignore that. It is only the caress of true love.'"

"So, it's a lie? I thought your kind couldn't lie."

"It's not entirely a lie. They are fated because we chose to make fate so. And if this is your way of hinting that you hope fate will bind us as a pair, then I can only say that while I am flattered at your regard, you will have to make your choice the old mortal way."

He smirked at me as if he really thought I wanted him. I felt blood rushing to my face but I refused to let him make me feel embarrassed.

With deliberate slowness, I spat out the bars of the cage. Of course, he turned a simple question into something self-aggrandizing! As if I would ever marry a Fae! A horrific, monstrous Fae!

The unicorn trotted down the hill and we lost the sharp, spectacular view as we descended into the tangled warmth of willows. Wings flapped as night birds fled our path. Maybe they'd seen how Scouvrel treated animals in his vicinity.

"Now that you have that foolishness out of your system, perhaps you'd like some *useful* knowledge?" Scouvrel said.

In the spirit world, I saw the plumy glow around the tangled willow trees ahead and a narrow path that burrowed through the archway of their tangled branches.

Scouvrel leaned forward as he urged the unicorn into the tangle, his figure wickedly sleek like a highwayman from one of the books I read in school.

And what did he look like here without my spirit vision? Did he look more beautiful than that?

I took a deep breath and pulled the blindfold up.

A scream bubbled up in my throat and I snapped my jaw shut.

I'd caught sight of the unicorn first. And with my blindfold up – seeing the real world through it – the unicorn was nothing but bones with strips of ragged, rotting flesh clinging to them and waving in the air. Flags in a brisk wind. Ragged flesh streamed from the boney horn jutting from its skull like a pennant. The creature's eye was nothing but a black empty hole. Dark, sticky fluid stained the ragged flesh around it. A glimmer of white bone peeked out from the back depths.

I yanked the blindfold down before I could see anything else, my whole body shaking in tremors of horror.

"Kill it," I whispered. I yanked my bow from my quiver and restrung it despite the rocking of the cage.

"You need to think of new solutions to your problems," Scouvrel said, bemused. "Killing isn't *always* the answer. For starters, it's a long walk and the unicorn is a convenient captive. Besides, the head tax on this one would be steep. He's from the Court of Cups, you know. Would you like me to owe your sweet sister a head tax? She might demand you as payment."

I fitted an arrow into the bowstring as Scouvrel lifted the cage to look at me and I fired. I missed his eye by an inch. That rocking motion was terrible for my aim.

"Your arrows have little use when you're the height of a beer mug," he said arrogantly, his lips curling upward in mockery. "But I applaud the effort."

He plucked the arrow from his face and tossed it at me. A tiny pinprick of blood welled up by his eye – not even enough to bother brushing away.

Frustrated, I scooped up my arrow, wiped it on the dirty handkerchief on the floor of the cage and then returned it and the bow to my quiver. I'd need a different way to fight my battles. My arrows really were no good here.

I reached for the blindfold again. I'd seen the unicorn. What could be worse than that?

"I'm much worse," Scouvrel breathed in promise, still holding the cage up so that all I could see was his eyes. I grabbed my bow and one of my arrows, fumbling to nock the arrow.

He laughed and held the cage out, striking a noble pose as if to tempt me to fire. I slid roughly across the floor, through the unicorn blood and mud and smashed into the bars on the other side. I wiped my hands on my breeches as I stood up again. He wouldn't see me cower.

"How can the unicorn bleed when it has no flesh?" I asked. My voice was hoarse.

"How do any of us bleed?" Scouvrel mocked. "How do any of us die? You have a lot to learn, Little Nightmare."

Very helpful.

I jammed my bow and arrow back into my quiver, steeled myself and reached for the blindfold again.

"How about a bargain," Scouvrel purred. His dark eyes flashed silver in the Faewald light. "Make a deal with me, Little Hunter. You don't need to see the Faewald through that blindfold of yours, but you do need some other things. Clean clothes, maybe? Another kiss? You seemed to like that last time."

"You really don't want me to see the real you in the Faewald, do you?" I asked, putting my free hand on my hip so I could glare at him more effectively.

The real him in my world had been feral and foxy, not at all the god-like beauty his glamor projected. How could he be any worse here?

He laughed. "Let's just say that I have secrets I'd like to keep. You'll buy those only with the steepest of prices."

I felt a little shiver of delight at his laughter. I couldn't help it. I wanted to know all his secrets.

And yet. If I didn't look at this world clearly, then I'd have no chance to find my way through it back to where my father suffered, nailed to a tree. No amount of secrets or bargains or tempting possibilities could be allowed to cloud my mind to that – to what I was really here for.

I was not here for power or secrets, not for thrills or delights, or even for satisfying my curiosity. I was here for my father. I didn't dare forget that.

"Then you should be afraid," I said. "Because I like to slay secrets."

I pulled the blindfold up before he could stop me.

I wasn't ready.

But I didn't scream even though the scream I suppressed ripped through my mind like a saw.

Scouvrel didn't look mortal. He didn't even look Fae. He looked like something crawling up from the depths of hell.

Tangled and wrapped, he was like a wreath made of writhing black willow branches that ended in ragged, moving endings. A reddish glow emanated from within the tangle – a wrathful fire that never ended. It looked agonizingly painful and he flinched and shuddered every time the tangle of his body rearranged itself. I tried to make out precisely where the waving ends of his tangled pieces ended, but they seemed to fade into nothing and it was hard to tell where they still had some physical sway and where they were nothing but dissolving spirit.

It was as if he was nothing but raw nerve endings forever exposed to the elements, torn and ravaged by winds I couldn't see. He was tangled and gnarled, a twisted thing of emotion and passion, ambition and cruelty with no hope of being anything else.

I swallowed down bile and a black terror like nothing I'd ever felt before. My knees were so weak that I gripped the cage to stay standing.

I wrenched the blindfold from my eyes with the last of my strength.

I gasped when his glamor returned – his soft, full lips turned up into a bitter smirk.

"Told you so."

Chapter Three

When I was six my father would sit me down in the fresh snow and ask me to duplicate every animal track I knew. Every day, he would add a track I didn't know.

"You can't be a good hunter unless you know the animals better than they know themselves, Allie. Ghouls, too. They're just as important to know. Watch everything they do. Everything has a pattern – a way they live, what they want, where they sleep, what they eat. Learn the pattern and you learn the prey."

I'd learned the prey.

But some things you have to hunt are too terrifying to want to know.

Chapter Four

My teeth chattered no matter how hard I tried to make them stop. He wasn't ... well, I knew he wasn't mortal. He was a monster.

I hadn't believed him when he was trying to tell me that.

Well, I had ... and yet I hadn't believed it like I believed it now.

My instincts had been wrong.

He was a monster. The unicorn was a monster. This whole world was a hellscape. I didn't dare look at the rest of it. My blindfold was very firmly pulled down around my neck, my eyes fixed on the velvet embrace of the night the way a sentenced man might stare at his executioner.

Come on, Allie! Find your fire. You're better than this. So, they're worse than anything you imagined? So what? You're a Hunter and you *hunt*. And the greater the predator, the more necessary the kill.

"You live forever?" I asked between chattering teeth. Forever. Like this. Twisted and tangled with all his ends unraveling.

"They call us immortal, don't they?" he asked lightly. His eyes were scanning the ghostly willows, a frown biting deep into his face. He paused. "I suppose it is a kind of immortality. Though most people would call it hell and consider it a miserable existence."

Should I be horrified? Should I pity him?

I felt as tangled as he had looked.

I kept on guard, slightly crouched against the bars, unwilling to let my guard down for even a moment.

"And now I must make a demand," Scouvrel said quietly.

"No demands," I said, finally getting my shaking under control. "Bargains go both ways."

His chuckle was delighted, but he kept his voice low, his eyes scanning above, below and all around as if he expected to be attacked from any direction.

"Fine. A bargain. You will be my ally in thwarting your sister and ... others. And in exchange, I will teach you how to fight like a Fae."

"Seems like a poor bargain," I whispered back. "Since I already know how to fight Fae. I beat you, didn't I?"

He rolled his eyes. "You have conquered my soul and planted your flag in my heart, and yet, surprisingly, that has not brought the Faewald to its knees. Where is my Hunter? Where is the one who swore to make us all pay?"

"You *will* pay," I hissed. "I will still make you *all* pay. This cage only limits me for now."

"That's my nightmare. Hold onto that fire! Bargain?"

I thought about it. From what I could tell so far, the Fae were dangerous and devious. Beating them would require everything I had to offer. And Scouvrel was the only piece I had access to in this game. I'd rather play with a pawn in my hand than a knave, but any piece at all was better than nothing.

"Agreed," I hissed. "I will be your ally."

"And I will teach you to fight like a Fae. Did you know that there are five words that come from the ancient mortal word wrae?"

We turned a corner in the tunnel of twisted trees. They moved constantly – just like him. And when they moved, the paths around us turned and twisted and reshaped themselves. There was no way I'd be able to find my way back through them without a map or a guide. Assuming I could get out of the cage.

"I had no idea," I said, letting my tone drip with disinterest.

"One became the word 'Fae.' How odd that you are the ones to name us, don't you think?" Scouvrel asked as he paused the unicorn's movement.

The path here branched in several directions and as the unicorn turned in place, I couldn't tell which way we had come from or which we were going. One of the paths grew over with blue tangled willows as I was watching. Another one opened a little way away and a flash of red caught my attention. Was that blood? An owl hooted in the velvet darkness and I shivered.

"The other four aren't like it at all." He paused. "We're being followed." Scouvrel drew the needle-sword from where he'd stashed it in his belt. It glowed brightly in the blue light of the woods.

"Assassins?" I asked.

"Perhaps. You'll learn that I'm always being followed. I draw interest like a sunset draws artists."

"Why is that?" I asked, wiping my hands on my trousers again. They were damp with sweat and if there was going to be action, I didn't want them to slip.

"Who can say? Perhaps it's because I'm so delightfully charming. Or perhaps it is my renowned beauty."

He was gorgeous – like a moonbeam come alive to ride with me, like the waving arms of a stately pine, or the full moon winking down on me, like the pleasant lapping of a summer lake, or smooth silk drawn across the skin. I shoved that thought aside and tried to remind him of his place.

"Yes, you're *all* gorgeous. How nice for you. As if beauty is anything more than a fleeting fancy, an illusion of value spread out indiscriminately."

"Bold words, Little Captive. I don't think you believe them."

His laugh was wicked.

He selected a path – the one with the trail of blood, which wasn't at all reassuring, and the unicorn thundered ahead.

I held on to the bars as the branches whipped around us, smacking the cage as often as not.

"The next word is wraith. Which – you'll admit – is pretty close to Fae," he said as we fled down the path. "You saw that when you pulled that blindfold up, didn't you?"

I tried not to shiver at the memory. Yes, wraith seemed accurate. The trees shifted again, and our path was blocked.

Scouvrel cursed.

An arrow hit the tree beside us with a *thunk*.

Really? They were shooting at us? They must really hate him. And they must really want me.

I narrowed my eyes as I assessed the shaft – still quivering in the tree. It was too short for a longbow and the fletchings too trim. It was no longer than my hand – when I wasn't miniature – vibrating like it was trying to sing. Crossbow.

I spun in the cage, but the neck of the unicorn blocked my view. It reared, screaming a horsey-scream and this time, Scouvrel leapt from its back as it bucked, landing on his feet in the snow with my cage in one hand and his needle-turned-sword in the other.

The unicorn leapt over us in a majestic arc, a quarrel sunk deep in its haunches as it thundered away. Great. It had been bad enough to have that thing carrying us. Having no mount at all while we were being hunted – that seemed worse.

"I'll miss that aberration," Scouvrel said wistfully. His fingers fit perfectly through the eye of the brass needle. He brandished it in front of us as if to ward off evil. I clung to the bars of my cage with both hands as the world around me spun and rocked. There was nothing I could do except clench my jaw and hold on for the ride.

"The next word, is wreath. Do you make wreaths in the mortal world? We make them here."

Something dark dropped from the trees above us.

"Care to make a bargain?" Scouvrel offered the attacker, but the man was silent. His face was covered with a golden mask but his ears were pointed and sharp. Fae to the core. No wings, though. He glowed a faint burgundy color as he slid through the shadows toward Scouvrel, brandishing a pair of knives.

Scouvrel lunged, his pin darting into the body of a second attacker. This man – a fae with small goat horns – wore a black mask with a beak nose and black feathers around the eyes, but in one hand he held a rapier-like sword. With the other, he flung a small crossbow into the trees, spinning as he deflected Scouvrel's lunge and tried to duck under his guard.

"No bargain?" Scouvrel's voice was a hiss. "How about a game? I like games."

Scouvrel lashed out with the cage and I yelled. "I'm still in here!"

I hit the bars painfully as the cage struck something solid. My head smashed into it and I gasped, recovering just enough to cling to the nearest bar with all my might as my feet were swept out from under me and the cage was pulled through the air in the other direction. My pack slipped from my back and hit the wall of bars with a smack. I risked a glance behind me and saw the attacker holding his head with his hand. Scouvrel had hit him with the cage.

Was he kidding? I wasn't a weapon!

My head rang with pain and stars danced across my vision.

But I'd never seen men fight men before – or Fae fight Fae. It was not the same as the hunt. It was not the acknowledgment of predator and prey. It was messy and filled with gasping breaths and grunts. Steam rushed off grappling bodies and from open wounds. Everything seemed to be a rush of action and determined violence.

"The next word," Scouvrel said between grunts, "is wrath. That's what I'm exhibiting here."

The sound of metal on metal brought a scream up in my throat and I barely bit it back as a blade as thick around as I was darted through the cage just a bar's gap away from me. The cage twisted mercilessly, and I lost my hold, falling through the air and crashing into the bars on the opposite side. My belly lurched as if I was still moving even as the cage kept falling through the air and landed with a bone-jarring thump. The sword was still wedged between the bars.

They thought they needed a sword to kill me? They could kill me with a pin right now!

My whole body was ringing. Pain dazzled me as I fought through it.

I took a moment to lean my head out of the cage and be sick into what appeared to be the moss around a tree root. Little blue flowers sprouted up through my vomit. Ugh. Gross.

But my flame was back. I shoved nausea into it and fear, too. Feed the fire! Fuel me! I will not die because some fool doesn't know how to use a sword. This isn't how Allie Hunter goes down.

Scouvrel's needle-sword was red with blood. He was standing on the corpse of the attacker wearing the bird mask. Two more assassins fought him.

"Get them!" I called. I needed out of this cage. I needed access to a proper bow and arrows. Or even that crossbow. "Show them all this so-called superiority of yours!"

They danced around each other with exquisite grace. Their fight seemed more like a dramatic dance than a breathless battle. They were all – including Scouvrel – dressed like royalty. Their clothing was perfectly fitted, perfectly stitched, perfectly adorned with braiding and embroidery and lace. A maroon cup was embroidered on each coat.

They were all beautiful – of course – would I ever meet a Fae who wasn't? Perfect specimens of masculinity, their muscles rippling gloriously any time they were revealed, their faces immortally lovely. Even when they snarled at one another it was the snarl of a great predator – elegantly violent – and not the ugly slur I would have seen on the face of a mortal.

I dared to lift the blindfold for a second and immediately regretted it. Open mouths ridged with rows of teeth slathered and snapped as the tangled creatures' flesh roiled over their bones, weaving and unweaving in blackened cords around their frames, the ends of the cords frayed and wispy as if disappearing into the spirit world.

I ripped the blindfold back off and tried to catch my shaking breath. Come on, Allie, fight it! Looks can't kill. Beauty is nothing but an illusion. And that means ugliness is, too. They can't kill you just by looking scary.

"And last of all," Scouvrel called to me, "is writhe. Which is what my enemies shall display."

Scouvrel ran a second Fae through, tossing his body aside as if it meant nothing. The dead Fae landed not far from me, beautiful face seeming to lose its beauty as he twisted in pain, the life fading from his eyes until he was only a wasted, starved, pale thing with too-sharp features and a feral foxy face. His hair was matted, and his clothing was nothing but rags. Just like when they were in our world.

The Fae were glamor on glamor, illusion on lie, tangled messes of deception.

Scouvrel cursed and I looked up just in time to see a sword plunging toward me. I lifted a hand on instinct. Stupid, Allie. Like my miniature hand could deflect a sword.

The blade stopped just as the point bit into my hand. I stepped back, cradling my palm. An agonizing red gash pierced all the way through my hand. I sucked in a breath around the flaring pain. The sword tip had missed the bones. That meant it could heal. It just hurt so much. So very much.

I stumbled backward and landed on my bottom, choking back pained gasps. I reached into my pocket and drew out my clean handkerchief winding it around the wound. It was already soaked with blood before I'd finished.

The sound of rasping metal made me look up. Scouvrel drew the swords from my cage, shoving them into their scabbards. He'd buckled two of the scabbard belts crosswise over his chest so that the swords hung over his back like a pirate from a book. His black hair tumbled loose to frame the troubled look on his face. He held the cage up so close to his face that I could see a tiny tattoo on his ear – the mark of a feather curving up along the edge of it to the very point.

"Still with me, Little Hunter?" his voice as almost a growl.

"I don't think they're hunting you for your grace and beauty," I said dryly. "In fact, I get the distinct impression that they wanted to end your life."

"And what a life it is," Scouvrel said with a wink.

He searched the bodies, rifling through their belt pouches and pockets. I eyed the maroon goblets stitched to their coats suspiciously. Court of Cups? Why send masked assassins and then label them like that? It made no sense. Unless it was a message.

"Who are they?" I asked.

"Enemies," he said. But he didn't sound too worried. "What would life be without enemies?"

"Able to continue?" I suggested.

"Dull," he said with a terrifying smile. "And I am never dull. Ready to play a fun game, Little Nightmare? The opening move of this game was just played and now I have the initiative. What shall we do with it? Shall we show them the meaning of the name *Fae*?"

Chapter Five

I clung to the cage with my good hand, pain shooting through my injured hand at every jostle and shake as Scouvrel climbed up through the willows, branches clawing at both of us as he worked his way higher and higher. They bent and sprang under his weight, bouncing us with every shift of his feet.

"Where are we going?" I whispered, gasping as the cage rocked against a stubborn branch.

"Tell me, Little Captive," Scouvrel said, leaning in to spare me a wicked smile. "How does it feel to be swinging around inside that cage? Do you feel the penance you're serving for keeping me locked inside a cell?"

"Is that what this is? Revenge?" I hissed. "Because I don't seem to be the only one who would like to lock you up."

"Oh, the assassins?" Scouvrel said, plunging up through the tops of the trees and into the wind howling above. "That's just a typical night in the Faewald. I do hope you're not saying it was dull. Your entertainment is among my primary concerns."

The stars above us were brighter than on earth. And they were moving. Not like shooting stars, just moving like they were dancing together rather than keeping steady guard over the worlds beyond.

"Are the stars alive?" I gasped, so awed that I forgot myself for a moment.

"Or are we *dead*?" Scouvrel asked back, his own eyes flicking up to the stars and his face a picture of delight for a bare half-second before he shifted his position like a lion preparing to lunge and then leapt.

I caught the scream before it erupted in my throat.

What in the ...?

He was leaping from branch to branch – branches far too light to hold him! He was like a songbird fluttering from twig to twig, almost magical in how he moved with their sway and spring rather than against them. His smile told me he was enjoying himself, lost in the fun of his movement.

I'd almost forgotten that he had wings – wicked things that looked like tangled pillars of wood smoke. Just looking at them unfurled and catching the wind made my heart catch in my chest. Once my father had burned a pile of brush as high as the house when he was helping Barrowrow clear a field. Flames had tangled into the black smoke, tints of orange and red braiding through the white and charcoal streams. Scouvrel's wings were just like that.

What kind of creature was so utterly gorgeous and horrific all tangled into one?

My heart was in my throat, but I fed that to the fire. Now was my chance to scout.

"How do you like the Tanglewood?" Scouvrel asked. "A good place for an ambush. But clearly not good enough. If you want to learn to fight like a Fae, then here's a good lesson: don't choose the obvious."

"I thought *they* were Fae," I snapped back.

"*Were* Fae, Little Captive. Had *they* learned to fight like Fae they might still be alive."

From up here, I could see the haunted wraith-like forest spreading out across the land, glowing lights twinkling among the branches and to a thick, rolling sea glimmering in the moonlight beyond the waving branches. The Tanglewood, he'd called it. It wasn't endless. It had just felt like that when I was inside it.

I shouldn't be seeing any of this without my blindfold on. I should only be seeing pale outlines.

But the rules here seemed to work differently. If I was being honest, I wasn't sure that any of this was real at all. Maybe I had died back there when the unicorn charged at me on the other side of the magic circle. Maybe this was some kind of hell meant to punish me for failing my sister, my father and my town.

Maybe it was my chance to destroy the Faewald utterly.

Frustration boiled up inside me, getting worse by the second as we fled from unknown shadows. Every bit of instinct I had was roaring up inside me demanding that I run and leap and fight. And I was trapped in this little cage like a flying squirrel tempted into a box. My father had caught one of those in the night for me when I was barely seven just to show me the night creature. He hadn't let me touch it or keep it no matter how much I begged.

"Capture is the worst kind of torture. All things long to be free," he'd said.

I was longing to be free and with every leap Scouvrel took, the longing was stronger.

My father was probably feeling the same way. I must not forget that.

"Are there more assassins out there?" I asked eventually, trying to keep my mind off how very trapped I was.

"Always." He ducked low this time so that his leap brought us within the cover of the branches. They were growing broader, the trees larger and larger as we went. "We must pass through a little town on the edge of the Tanglewood. It's the only way through this part."

"Can't you just fly over it?"

"Not without drawing the eye of every Fae in the area."

"One of them put his blade through my hand," I said, holding my bloody palm up. It really did hurt. It needed stitching and a real bandage.

Scouvrel laughed. "Then I'm glad I killed him, Little Captive. You belong to me now, and any harm to you is a theft from me. Here's your next lesson: If you must go somewhere you don't want to go, pretend to like it."

I snorted. Ahead, there was a bright yellow glow as if from lanterns. We bobbed toward it, seeming to speed up.

"Is that the little town?" I asked.

"Tanglewood Market," Scouvrel agreed.

"Is this your home? Will they try to kill you here?"

This time, his laugh tinkled like a glass tapped by a knife. "It's the Faewald, Little Captive. If no one is trying to kill you, then you aren't even in the game."

"What game?"

I was trying to catch his eye, but carried at his waist level, all I could really see was his jacket and his bare torso under it, whenever the jacket slipped to the side. I was pretty good at reading people, but even I couldn't read a man's mind by looking at the muscles of his midsection.

"The Game of Courts, Little Captive. They want to capture the Knave."

"And that's you?" I'd heard Hulanna call him that.

"One and the same." It sounded like he was smirking.

"What Court do you belong to?"

"None. The Knave is not of a Court. He is one of four players who march to their own beat, who live and die outside the Courts of Fools. The Knave – that's me. The Sooth – you met her. The Balance. The Kinslayer. We're an essential part of the game, but the price is loneliness. No Court. No family. No home. Just the game forever and always."

"Why did you choose to become the Knave if you hate it so much?" I asked. The more I talked, the less I had to think about the fiery ache in my hand or the nausea that rippled over me as my cage bobbed back and forth wildly.

"The usual way. I killed the old Knave. Just like, eventually, one of these fools will kill me."

"I thought you were immortal," I said snidely.

"We practically are – unless we're murdered. You won't catch a Fae dying of illness or old age."

I paused. "Is that because you're so hearty or because most people are murdered before illness or old age even have a chance?"

His laugh held no humor. "Clever question, Little Captive. Which answer would please you best?"

Would I feel better knowing he could die at any moment or better knowing he might live and keep me captive for a very long time?

"I don't know," I said eventually.

"Neither do I," he admitted. "And now, let's find a place to hide. Night is waning. We'll be caught and killed if we're out after the sun rises."

"Even the great Knave?"

"Most especially a prize like me."

In the distance, the sounds of people were plain. A party was winding down. Scouvrel angled toward the voices, hunched over his side slightly.

"Were you hurt in the battle?" I asked, surprised by my own concern.

"No more than you were." His words were clipped, and his eyes never left the glowing light ahead. "Don't talk to anyone in the market."

"What are you going to do with me?" I asked, sharply, suddenly nervous by the appearance of a settlement. The last Fae party I'd seen had featured my father being tortured for entertainment and my sister doing the torturing. What would this one be like?

"I'm going to sell you to the highest bidder," he said lightly.

I gasped. "But I'm your ally!"

"Exactly."

My belly seemed to fall into a pit. As wicked as Scouvrel was, I'd never considered that a different Fae might hold me captive. The thought made me break out in a cold sweat. That would be ... torturous.

"Right now?" I choked out.

He laughed. "Eventually. When it suits my purpose."

"You lie."

"I never lie," he reached a finger in the cage and flicked me lightly. "I told you that."

What did you say to that? Captured – and potentially for sale. I felt ... small. Even smaller than I already felt inside this cage. And I was furiously angry. He thought he could sell *me*? Really? Like I was a hare caught in a trap?

The town – if that was what it was, was full of laughter and screams. One warm shadowed burrow in the wrapping willows was connected by a close squeeze to the next and so on and so on. The first burrow held a long bar where a Fae with greenish skin and white whiskers offered us a steaming mug of something that went *glop*. Mortal skulls lined the walls in stacks as high as the ceiling and the patrons drank from chipped teacups – none of them matching. My eyes widened. Was Scouvrel going to sell me to a Fae like that? Would I spend my days in a cage on a bar while Faeries drank from unmatched porcelain?

Scouvrel ignored his offer – to my relief – squeezing past a woman with deer antlers and flushed cheeks who tried to steal a kiss from him. She wore a necklace of emeralds and fingerbones. Maybe he'd sell me to a woman like that for more kisses and I'd find myself under a discarded dress on her bedroom floor. I shivered. Perhaps I should make a bargain with Scouvrel. But what should I ask for that would keep me from being the plaything of these creatures?

We went on through a burrow that sold only masks in every color and design I could imagine. Some without holes for eyes and some with holes for three or four eyes. The shops and bars and apothecaries ran one into the other in little caves woven into the willows or packed with large downy feathers like birds' nests. Each more subtly creepy than the last.

One seller proclaimed she could make Scouvrel's toes curl with the scent of her perfumes. Her hair was braided with beads that looked like eyeballs. They were glass – I was sure, but that didn't make them more appealing.

Another suggested Scouvrel could pass the night in blissful illusions with a single taste of silver powder. His sickly face and gaunt frame suggested the opposite.

A third – a man who wouldn't leave a shadowy door from which horrified screams rang out like a cantata of terror, offered Scouvrel a love potion, sure to draw the eye of any maiden he desired.

"Ah, but I already have the full attention of the only one I need," he said slyly which made the seller's companion – a deliciously pretty Faerie woman dressed in brown and green patches that did nothing to hide her pleasant figure – sigh lightly and bite her bottom lip until he growled. But still, he moved on.

Really? Wicked Scouvrel liked flirting women who bit their lips? I'd thought better of him than that. Not that it mattered to me in any way.

Someone was drumming on a set of metal buckets and Fae were dancing and dueling, juggling and playing cards, flirting and drinking, buying and selling. But there was no other music and it made the rest of their behavior feel like a farce. Like someone who was humming a song they'd forgotten the words to, or brandishing a sword without knowing it could kill.

"Do they party all night?" I whispered as Scouvrel ducked behind a shop, climbing the willow branches furtively, watching often over his shoulder.

"In the Faewald, we sleep during the day," he whispered back, his whisper gave me a little thrill I couldn't explain. "Didn't anyone ever tell you that monsters only come out at night?"

"Then maybe we should travel during the day," I suggested.

"Don't you want that hand tended before it festers?" he countered. It was hard to argue with that.

"Your Fae villages are awfully small and simple considering all the bragging you've done. Here I thought I'd be amazed. But actually, I'm left feeling disappointed. My village is twice what that one is," I said, disguising my horror at the place with flippancy. I'd rather burn it to the ground than ever live there. Someone probably should do just that.

He scowled at me, but there was amusement in his eyes. "The Tanglewood Market is nothing but a backwater market for the dregs of Fae society. If you'd been impressed, I would have thrown your cage in the river. But don't tempt me. I could sell you down there for a pair of sparrows and leave. Would you like that fate?"

I crossed my arms sullenly.

"I'm worth more than sparrows!"

I was not used to bargaining from a place of such weakness. What could I offer him to get what I wanted? Because I didn't want to be sold. As wicked as Scouvrel was, he was a known evil. A known evil who killed three people tonight without thinking twice about it – but yes, known. And I didn't want to be sold to a man drinking in a bar.

My heart was hammering in my chest at the thought of it. Sweat formed along my brow.

Scouvrel slipped through the branches, doubling back twice and taking a circuitous route that eventually led to a tight squeeze through a matted roof of branches and mud and into what seemed like a nest for a bird – a very large, man-sized bird. Glass buoys hung from bits of twine around the tangled branches and tiny lights guttered inside them. One side of the branches parted to a mossy ledge, and a babbling brook tumbled beside it, coating everything in a cool spray of water.

Downy white feathers lined the floor and curled up the walls of willow branches which had been carved by someone with an enormous amount of patience. They had carved stories scene by scene into the wood of the willows so that one could lie on the feathers and look up at the walls and ceiling and read an entire story in the pictures there. It was ... strangely inmortal. Almost as if someone had been imprisoned here and carved these things to pass the time. But there were no bars or locks. One could easily slip into the brook beyond. So why take the time to carve these branches?

"Is this your home?" I asked warily. It seemed oddly simple. Homey, even.

Scouvrel laughed. "Hardly. But everyone needs a hole to hide in from time to time. We'll stay here for today."

"And then will you sell me for a pair of sparrows?" I challenged him. "You are *not* going to sell me, Scouvrel."

His expression twisted with something that might have been sorrow before he changed the subject. "Bargain with me, Little Captive. Bargain with me, and I will stitch and bandage your hand and let you wash before you have to go back in the cage."

"Maybe I want my freedom," I protested. Start high, Allie. That's how bargaining works.

"I'm afraid I won't bargain for that." The look in his eyes was wicked. "I enjoy you in my power far too much."

"I thought we were friends," I said frustration making my mouth twist in anger.

He sobered, looking at me with a piercing expression but saying nothing. He sat down on the feathers, slipping off his boots and coat and lying back into the feathery down. A long scrape ran down his ribs and feather tattoos wrapped around one side of his rib cage, brushing against knives, playing cards and something that looked like a mouse skull.

He pulled my cage so he could see me easily as he crossed his arms behind his head. My eyes drifted to the corded muscles of his arms and torso and the sensual way the feather tattoos wound around his forearms, but all I really saw was the memory of him in this world as he really was, twisted, agonized and inmortal.

He was gorgeous and horrifying. Lovely and awful.

I swallowed. "Then don't sell me. Bargain with me for that. I don't want to be sold."

His tone was heavy as a rock. "I must sell you to the highest bidder, Allie. I can't play the game any other way. We'll bargain for something else."

Fuel, Allie. Let your fear fuel you.

"You don't own me."

"Don't I?" his smirk was taunting, but he watched me with a calculating look in his eye as if he was planning something.

"If I make a bargain with you," I said, licking my lips, his eyes lit up and he sat up so suddenly that I fell backward from the bars.

"Yes?"

"If I make a bargain with you," I started again, straightening and holding my head high, my arms crossed over my chest, "what would you want on your end."

He smirked, pursing his lips as he looked me over. I felt my cheeks heating.

"You aren't as lovely as your sister, you know," he said and an old bitterness as old as I was, reared up inside me.

"Tell me something I don't know," I muttered.

"Challenge accepted." There was an excited light in his eyes as he thought for a moment. "Beauty is no accomplishment. That's something you don't seem to know."

"I'm pretty sure that I just told you that a few hours ago."

"Ah, but you didn't mean it. I do. Beauty is something you stumble on in the dark – a chance gift given by the Great Judge. Cruelty on the other hand, well that's something you can culti-vate."

"Since you have both, I suppose you're doubly blessed," I said dryly.

His laughter was genuine. "Do I? How generous of you to say so. I suppose that I *am* doubly blessed."

He turned his back on me, stood up, and pulled one of the willow branches ringing the nest like it was a lever. To my sur-prise, the branches parted and revealed a closet. He reached in and almost without thought, he pulled out fresh boots, tight trousers and a black silk shirt with a high collar. He paused over the jackets, choosing a jacket of a vibrant bottle green. It was uncut velvet on which someone had embroidered fanciful black feathers with silver tips.

"Here's your next lesson in fighting like a Fae. Craft the per-fect image."

"Don't you think you should look a bit more manly?" I frowned. "That's a lot of lace I'm seeing."

His eyes narrowed. "Manly? I suppose I could arrive naked, adorned in nothing but the blood of my foes, but I prefer something with a collar."

He tossed them to the side and began to strip.

I gasped and turned my back until I heard a splash in the creek beyond. When I spared him a nervous glance, he laughed again. The water covered him up to the waist, but he still looked completely indecent. He would look indecent if he wore a dozen layers of clothes from toe to chin. There was just something about him that wore indecency like a badge of honor.

"You're living in my world now, Little Captive," he said. "Until you realize that, you'll be nothing but a prisoner in a little cage."

Unacceptable.

"I'll bargain with you," I said, jutting my chin up into the air. "Tell me what you want."

Chapter Six

His eyes lit with excitement and he reached out of the water to snatch up my cage and put it on his knees. He was wearing trousers after all, to my relief.

He leaned back against a mossy rock and let the water swirl around him as his smile deepened. I glanced down at the bubbling brook. Water swirled a breath below the cage. One slip from him and the cage would fall into the water and I'd die here under the waves. I looked a little deeper and gasped. Was that hair swirling just under the bubbles? I almost thought I could make out the face of a woman far into the depths of the creek, but it couldn't be that deep.

"Seeing your fate in the water?" Scouvrel teased. "They say that the clear of sight can see the girls who have drowned here if they look carefully."

"What girls?" I asked, keeping my tone light even as my eyes found another woman's outline, her hair swirling up and tangling around Scouvrel.

"The dryads of this creek are vengeful," he said with a shrug. His eyes never left me as he spoke, as if somehow I was more fascinating than what he was talking about. "They drown pretty women who come here out of jealousy."

"Then I should be safe enough," I said more blithely than I felt. "As no one has ever called me pretty."

He laughed.

"Let's bargain, Knave," I said, holding to my resolve. If I could not be free just yet, I at least did not want to be sold. And perhaps he wouldn't bargain for that, but maybe I could craft a bargain that came close.

"What would you like, Little Captive? I've already made you my ally and offered you my great wisdom on the world you've entered. What more do you want?" Scouvrel said, leaning back so that the water washed over his hair and then sitting up and shaking it like a dog might. A drop of water hit me in the face, and I scowled as I scrubbed the water away with my sleeve.

"I want to know what you're demanding first," I countered. "I'm not so foolish as to bargain with you without knowing what it's for."

"Oh, don't be so mistrusting, Little Captive. I've been a good friend to you. I brought you to the Faewald, didn't I? And you so wanted that. And I did try to keep you from seeing our world without the glamor. That was a kindness. You pain me with your suspicion."

"And what have you done to make me less suspicious?" I demanded.

He laughed. "What did you do when the tables were turned? You were everything a fierce little nightmare should be, so don't talk now of friendship and loyalty. Make me an offer and we shall see if I bite."

"I offer you," I began, and his lips parted as he held his breath. What did I have that he might want? "I offer you a game."

"A game?" he seemed pleased.

Okay, good. But what game could I offer him?

"Yes," I said, grasping for an idea. "You will let me out of this cage for the space of an hour, allow me to bathe and dress in clean, dry clothing, eat something, and you will heal my hand and in exchange, I will not try to escape for that single hour and I will give you a game."

His smile was utterly delighted.

"Oh ho, but your bargain has holes, Little Captive. Let's try it again. You," he said firmly, "will be allowed out of this cage for long enough to bathe and be bandaged – but then you will return to it without trying to escape, begging me to release you or in any other way trying to manipulate me into releasing you until you are back in the cage. You will not attempt to kill me or harm me in any way. I will offer you food, and a chance to bathe, but you will wear the clothing I give you *and* you must leave your old clothes in the cage."

"I don't think so!" I protested.

"You can use that disgusting rag on the floor to cover up. It needs to come out anyway," he said wrinkling his nose. "Besides, I'm not done. I will not heal your hand. You will bear that scar. However, I will stitch and bind your wound. In return, you will give me a kiss and a game."

"No kiss," I said. This was bad enough already.

He smirked. "Are my kisses so valuable that you hesitate to take one? Fine. No kiss. Do we have a bargain?"

"You didn't even ask me what game I'm offering," I protested.

"I expect you will be inventive," he said, delight filling his face. "Are we agreed?"

"Yes," I said, worried now that he was being so agreeable. I'd have to be very clever with this game if it was going to sway him. But I had a little time to think about it while I took care of necessities. Or... well, just because these bargains were binding for him it didn't mean that they were binding for me, right? "I agree to the bargain."

"I also agree to the bargain," Scouvrel said. "Now, get those dirty clothes off."

I scowled at him, grabbing the filthy cloth from the floor and arranging it around me so I could strip off my backpack, bow and quiver, and my filthy clothes under the cloak of what had once been one of my handkerchiefs and now was bigger than a bedsheet.

My cheeks were hot before I'd even begun, and his snickers were not helping.

"Let's do this," I said as soon as I'd stripped off all my worldly goods. I'd kept a knife in my hand under the cloth, though. Would he be able to tell?

He opened the cage door.

Chapter Seven

When I was eleven, I went for a walk with Olen in the woods. I liked walking with Olen. He never wanted anything in particular beyond your company.

We had wandered toward the cliffs near the river, when we heard a frantic calling in the distance. Olen had looked at me and neither of us had needed to say a word. We both knew we were going to help whatever creature was calling like that.

I'd seen eagles from afar, but I'd never seen one so close. Its talons were as long as my smallest finger.

"Easy," Olen had said as I slipped my jacket off. "Easy now."

The eagle was stuck in a crevice of rock. One wing was broken. It hung uselessly at its side as the eagle thrashed with its feet and the other wing, but the wing was pinned in the crevice and I wasn't even sure it could fly with just one wing. Above it, two ghouls hovered, waiting to steal its spirit.

"How do you think it got like that?" I asked but Olen just shook his head. We never did get a satisfactory answer. Some things just happen.

I snatched up a long stick and leapt toward the ghouls, letting it smash through their spectral bodies. They snarled at me, but two more swipes sent them skulking away.

"I still don't' know how you do that," Olen said with a shiver. "The minute they look at me, I'm frozen in place!"

I grunted, throwing the stick to the side and gripping my jacket. I threw the jacket over the eagle's head so he wouldn't fight us, and Olen pulled him out of the rocks. With his talons and beak wrapped in my jacket, Olen carried him all the way home.

We set his wing together that afternoon, both nursing wicked cuts after we were done. The eagle had not trusted our healing ministrations.

I went out and trapped a squirrel to feed him while Olen put him in their goat shed. The eagle didn't touch the squirrel. But he did get used to the shed and when his splint came off and Olen set him free, he made his nest in a tree beside the goat shed and every spring he and his mate roosted there.

And when he saw Olen or me, he would tip his wing in greeting.

Some kindnesses tie a knot between two creatures that isn't easily cut.

Chapter Eight

I was unusually nervous as I slipped from the cage and grew to my full size and that made me furious. Why should I be nervous? He should be the one who was worried.

I stepped straight into the water, up to my waist already, and tried not to think about the drowned girls in the water or how I could almost feel their hair tangling around my feet. Around me, lily pads sprouted white flowers. Maybe they always did that at this time of day. I tried not to think about it. No distractions, Allie. This is your chance to escape.

On the other side of the creek, the tangled willows were waiting. All I had to do was stab Scouvrel, grab my stuff from the cage and run.

He set the cage down on the bank at the same moment I lunged for him with my dagger.

It stopped an inch from his body, my own arm locked against my will. My muscles wouldn't move.

I looked up at him horrified. What would he do?

He took one look at my face and doubled over in laughter. I grabbed the knife from my frozen hand with my free hand and tried again, but now the other hand was frozen. Scouvrel tried to speak, but his words were swallowed with laughter. He held up a hand – as if I could move anyway! – while he tried to stop laughing.

"What's so funny?" I demanded, my fury tasting bitter in my mouth. What had he done to me?

"You little nightmare," he said when his laughter finally faded, a wicked gleam in his eye. "You, delicious little nightmare! Your word might not be worth a copper penny in your world, but it binds you here as surely as mine binds me."

But he didn't seem upset. He took the knife from my hands almost affectionately and as soon as it was gone, my arms sagged at my side. I stole a longing glance at the willows beyond the creek. There would be no escape tonight. I felt tears pricking my eyes, but I *would not* cry. I forced them into my internal fire. More fuel.

"If you don't mind," I said icily, "I need to bathe."

My hand was killing me. It needed tending even more than I needed to clean myself, but one thing at a time.

"Do you ever," he agreed. "You stink of unicorn and rotting flesh."

I scowled and ducked into the water, disgusting mud-and-gore-covered sheet and all.

"Don't be modest on my account," Scouvrel teased.

I'd forgotten the effect he had on me when we were the same size. I'd forgotten how good his glamor made him look – the way my heart sped up despite the fact that my brain was screaming, 'You saw the real him, you idiot and he's nearly demonic!'

My heart didn't care. Neither did my lungs, apparently. I was struggling to breathe normally as my eyes caught every gleaming wet muscle when he pulled himself out of the creek and sauntered into the nest beyond.

"I'll just choose something interesting for you to wear, shall I?" he said.

"It had better be decent."

If it wasn't, we'd try another kind of violence. There had to be ways to get around that bargain.

A wisp of green silk flew out the door and landed on the mossy bank just as I was finishing unbraiding my hair.

"Is that what I'm supposed to wear?" I asked.

There was only laughter. I made a frustrated sound in my throat and ducked under the water, trying very hard to keep my eyes closed and not to think about dead girls. Something squelched under my feet. Something else tangled around my foot. I dropped the dirty cloth and ran to the creek bank with my knees as high as I could, trying desperately not to scream and not to touch the water again.

They'd been touching me. The dead girls had been touching me!

The scrap of silk turned out to be a light robe. I pulled it on just as Scouvrel was coming out of the nest wearing dry trousers and drying his wet hair with one hand. He'd shaved. How had he done that so quickly? He bit his lip when he looked at me.

"What?" I demanded, frowning.

"You're looking mortal."

"Unlike you, I look mortal *all* the time."

"Yes, and isn't that a magical little talent," he said. He was looking at my feet. Which should have been a relief since with his wicked tastes I would have expected his gaze to be somewhere else. I looked down at the clumps of bluebells blooming all around where I stood. Had those been there before?

"Let's deal with your hand," he said, laying out a green cloth on the moss and sitting down beside it. It was long and bottle green and looked nothing like a bandage. There was also a small brass needle and thread. "Stitches first."

I didn't want him to sew my hand, but just thinking of the needle going through flesh turned my stomach. I wasn't going to be able to do it myself.

"I wish you'd agreed to heal it," I said longingly, sitting down beside him and offering him my hand as I looked away. I winced as he poured something over the wound. I hadn't realized he'd had a flask with him. But it made sense. Alcohol was good for cleaning wounds.

"Ah, but then I couldn't do this," he said softly, sounding like he was actually enjoying himself.

I felt the needle bite my skin.

"You enjoy needlework so much?"

"Shhh, you're distracting me."

I bit my lip as he worked, cleaning and stitching. The minutes stretched out in painful silence. The feeling between us felt like the air before a lightning strike. I could almost taste the acid of it on my tongue.

"Hold onto that hand for a moment while I get the bandage ready," he whispered and my skin turned to gooseflesh.

I held my injured hand in the other palm. He was surprisingly good at stitching. His work looked neat and tidy, though my skin beneath it burned hot.

"Have you done this before?" I asked.

"Never." His eyes glinted and his smile was mischievous as he began to wind the green bandage around my hand. "But there's a first time for everything."

I was so caught in the gleam of mischief in his eyes that I hardly noticed what he was doing until I looked down.

"You're terrible at bandaging," I said. "You've tangled both our hands in that cloth. Do you *mean* to wrap it that way?"

"I do," he said, sounding so incredibly sincere that I laughed. He paused seeming to enjoy the moment before he spoke with a challenge in his eyes. "Do you think you know a better way?"

I repeated his words back to him wryly. "I do."

Triumph flashed through his expression along with barely concealed pleasure. After a moment, it softened and I gasped. Scouvrel was never soft. What had I said to bring this on? Shaking my head, I pulled my good hand free and finished wrapping the wound myself.

"Now," I said when I was done. "There were supposed to be clothes."

"Laid out on the bed," he said, coughing awkwardly. "And then you get back into the cage and explain this game."

The clothes, it turned out, were a tight pair of woven green leggings, a fanciful pair of golden sandals laced with red berries and silver leaves, a light tunic without sleeves made entirely of tiny downy white feathers and a short golden jacket sewn all over with brown iridescent eyes. I felt very strange in it. Like a wet eagle. Hopefully, my real clothing could be washed and dried before anyone else saw it.

"Whose clothes are these?" I asked.

"Mine," Scouvrel said. That had to be a lie. They fit me like a glove.

"Ready for your cage again?" Scouvrel asked, holding it up as I sauntered out of the closet where I'd dressed. He was flushed and a little breathless and I frowned, puzzled as he offered me a small bowl of nuts with the other hand. He shrugged. "It's all the food I had on hand."

"Are you ready to lose the game?" I replied. But I didn't take any nuts. The book had said to only eat food with salt. I certainly didn't want to be more trapped than I already was.

It's not forever, Allie. It's just for now.

You're clean, bandaged, and you learned you can't break your word. That's something, right? Cherish small victories.

"I won't be losing," Scouvrel said, latching the cage door and disappearing into the closet. "But we'll have to play tomorrow. We both need sleep."

He stepped out of the closet and it was my turn to gasp. He looked every inch of a Faerie knave as he strapped on a bandolier of knives and clipped a pair of golden earcuffs to one of his ears. A Fae knave who was planning to steal away with me into the forest.

"Don't break your rules on my account," I said wryly.

He rummaged in the closet again and came out with a pitcher, a pair of thimbles and a bowl. He filled them all with water in the creek, drank from the pitcher and then set the bowl beside my cage.

"Here. Have a drink, wash your clothes, whatever you need."

I didn't require any more encouragement. I untied my backpack, pulled out my tent and I was setting it up between the bars of the cage before he was finished drinking his water. I had a drink from a thimble, refilled my waterskin and had my clothes scrubbed and hanging from the bars of the cage by the time he pulled the cage close to his chest, wrapped his body around it and lay down.

"That's awfully close," I mumbled. It was far too awkward to look at his chest or legs curled around the cage, just out of reach of the iron bars.

"Don't want you stolen," he said, but his voice was faint and I thought he might already be asleep when he mumbled something that almost sounded like the word, "Precious."

But that was ridiculous. I waited as his face slowly softened and his breathing deepened. But I didn't slip into my tent. Oh no. Because I had the golden key in my hand. The key that I had forgotten I'd put in the backpack.

Chapter Nine

Maybe I should have felt guilty doing this. After all, I'd promised I would be Scouvrel's ally. And he'd been very nice about bandaging my hand, even with all that silliness about demanding I dress a certain way. But I was never meant to be caged.

And this was a magic key. It even still had the unicorn hair wrapped around it.

I'd have to leave my clothes and the tent. If I tried to take them, he might wake up though I could bring the pack with everything else.

With care, I strapped it onto my back and eased myself up to the latch on the cage. Trying to lift it was useless. There was no wire wound around it anymore. There was no keyhole. But I had a magic key. Surely it would do something. Carefully, I lifted the key to touch the latch. It fell open and I breathed a sigh of relief, stashing the key in my bag again and carefully slipping out into the night.

I was full size the moment I stepped from the cage.

I stole a look at Scouvrel. He looked so small now that I was larger than his hand. And so vulnerable with his dark lashes lying against his silky skin. I bit back sympathy. Since when had Scouvrel needed that from me? He could take care of his winged self just fine.

Without a second look over my shoulder, I stole out to the creek bank and crept along the mossy stones. I'd have to follow the creek out of the woods. I didn't know any other way out, but creeks always flowed to bigger bodies of water. I could follow it right out to the sea I'd seen on the way here.

I almost slipped my blindfold up. Don't do it, Allie. You know what's out there. Looking at it won't make it any easier.

I glanced over my shoulder. Each place I'd put a foot along the bank left a blossom of bluebells. Great. I was leaving a track of flowers in this crazy world. No wonder Scouvrel acted like he made the sun rise and set. When flowers bloomed wherever you walked, that could go to someone's head.

With a sigh, I stepped into the shallow part of the creek. No more flower prints. But it meant I had to walk through the swirling hair. With my heart in my throat, I crept through the water.

I was no stranger to clambering through the wilderness. And that was why I was worried. It would be dawn soon enough. Scouvrel said they slept during the day, but what if he turned in his sleep and noticed I was gone? In the light of day, it should be easy to notice. How far could I get before Scouvrel saw the empty cage? And would it be fast enough? Would I be able to hide?

Something smelled like woodsmoke.

There were people nearby somewhere. I needed to slow down and make as little noise as possible, so I wasn't caught. Was it getting warmer? I dabbed at my forehead. It was hot as summer.

Something crackled in the distance and I froze.

The smoke was getting thicker.

A faint orange light tinted the horizon. Not the gold of dawn – a dark orange, menacing glow.

Something bigger than a campfire was burning out there.

I froze, not sure which way to run. I had to stay in the creek. It was the one thing I knew wouldn't burn, though I might need to duck into the deepest part of it if the fire got this far.

The Tanglewood had seemed ancient. A fire like this one couldn't be normal, could it?

The glow seemed brighter ahead of me. If I kept going that way, I'd be sure to find the fire. But if I turned around, Scouvrel would be waiting. I'd rather bet on my own skill at survival in desperate circumstances than bet on his good graces.

Gritting my teeth, I pressed on. I was no one's captive.

Sweat slicked my brow and back. The orange light was getting brighter and so was the sky as dawn broke.

Maybe I should turn around. Maybe the creek wouldn't be enough protection. I'd seen animals burned to a crisp after a forest fire went through. I'd seen their young huddled under them safe from the flames. Would a creek give that much protection?

I was biting my lip, worried, when I suddenly saw actual flames. They roared toward me through the Tanglewood moving impossibly fast, licking at willows and dry grass in an all-consuming kiss of death.

I drew a deep breath and threw myself in the water.

I opened my eyes. Blank, unseeing eyes met mine and I screamed underwater as my nose met the nose of one of the dead girls. She was just as pretty as Scouvrel said she would be. And just as dead. Her hair swirled around me. I panicked, thrashing in the water.

And I smacked the floor of the cage, the last of the air knocked right out of my lungs.

"Ooof."

"What have you done to those lovely clothes?" Scouvrel said. "They looked so charming on you. Before."

But I didn't care that I was a mess of smoke and water. I cursed, leaping to my feet, but there was nothing I could do. I was small again. I was caged again.

I screamed in frustration. At least I still had the key, right?

No. My hand was empty. I gasped, my breath coming now in little panicked spurts as I felt all around me, searching, searching ...

"Looking for this?" Scouvrel asked, showing me the golden key, full-sized in his hand. He jammed it in his pocket. "Well, at least you know now. You can't escape. Not really. And now I need to break another rule."

"What rule?" I asked, shivering as the water pooled at my feet, the gorgeous clothes Scouvrel had given me soaking wet and bedraggled.

He looked serious – something he seldom was – and even as he spoke to me, he kept his eyes shaded by his hand as if he were afraid to look at the fire.

"We're traveling by day. I don't much fancy being burned alive. Your sister does delight in the dramatic," he said, grabbing my cage and leaping into the dawn.

Chapter Ten

"Shouldn't we go back to Tanglewood Market?" I asked. I hadn't liked that place, but it would still be better than a fiery forest.

"What do you think is burning? By nightfall, it will be nothing but ash and regret."

I tied my pack and quiver to the bars as Scouvrel leapt into the air. Last time we'd been fleeing assassins I'd been practically no use at all, but I wasn't going to be useless this time. I was the Hunter. I was not a victim no matter how caged I was.

That's what I had to hold onto. I wasn't a wandering captive. My fate hadn't been torn from my hands. I had to remember that. I couldn't let myself start believing I was a victim.

I was here to save my father and sort out things with my sister – whether that meant dragging her home by her hair and thrashing her for this foolishness or – something else.

And that meant I was a spy. It was up to me to gather every bit of information I could while I was in this cage. I had the perfect view of it all from here. I just needed to watch and wait like a good hunter did, keeping my eyes out for sign. Learning my prey until I could predict their every movement. Then, I could hunt again.

I couldn't afford to forget my purpose, even if I was wearing ridiculous soaking wet Faerie clothing and stuck in a cage. Once I had the backpack strapped in place, I gathered up my real clothing, hit them against the bars until the worst of the mud was off of them and strung them up across the other side of the cage to dry. They were soaking wet from Scouvrel's splashing at the creek – which was as close to "washed" as they were going to get.

Good. Settled.

By the time I was back to the bars, watching what we were doing, smoke was thick enough to make me wind my blindfold around my nose and mouth as I re-braided my red hair.

"Have fun swimming with the dead girls?" Scouvrel asked. "Lucky for us, you aren't pretty enough to drown."

"Yeah, lucky."

We were flying. That was why the ride had been so smooth. The breath caught in my lungs at the realization. I'd never been so high up before. And that meant I'd never had so far to fall.

We weren't very high in the sky, but we did zip between the trees, keeping ahead of the orange blaze. I tried not to be impressed. So, Scouvrel could fly on those smoke wings. So what? That didn't make him amazing. It made him a bird – sort of. And birds could be brought down with arrows.

"How did you get me back?" I asked.

"I thought of you as small."

I had no idea that could work both ways. I frowned. The next time I got out, I should try that on him. If I ever got out again. I shivered.

Why hadn't I thought of trapping him in the cage once I was free? All I'd been thinking of was my own freedom, but if I'd been paying attention, I would have realized I could have trapped him in the cage and saved myself from being caught again. Of course, that would mean that I'd be burning to death right now.

"What makes you think my sister set this fire?" I asked him.

In the distance, screams broke out and I tried not to think about who was dying in the blaze. This fire was not something I could do anything about. And these weren't my people. If I went around caring about what Fae did to each other I'd just be a ball of misery and that would accomplish nothing. But my heart lurched painfully in my chest at each scream that tore through the smoke and they built up until I felt like my own body was aflame with caring.

"She likes her games violent and quick. She's flushing us out," Scouvrel said. He carried me with his hand relaxed to his side so I could see very little of him unless I lay on my back in the cage and looked up. "Which reminds me, Little Hunter, you owe me a game."

I did owe him a game. But how did I craft one to get the most information out of him about our enemies? He wouldn't lie to me, but he often made the truth dance. Maybe if I knew how he really felt about things, I could find out what he really wanted. And then I could use that to get free. Plus, it would help in figuring out who was who when we met other Fae.

"It's a game like Truth and Lie, but a little different," I said, making it up as I went. The cage was getting hot as we maneuvered out of a gust of smoke and ash. I sat on my pack to try to keep the worst of the heat from the cage from bothering me. The wind was at our back, driving us before the flames and Scouvrel kept it there, refusing to glance even for a moment at the fire behind us. "When a situation comes up, you say how you feel on a scale of one to five. Five being the highest. So, if

I look back at the flames and ask you, 'Fear of burning?' you say?"

"One," he said, smiling. "The flames will not touch us, Little Nightmare. But how do we determine who wins?"

"You'll know if you win," I said because I had no idea and it seemed like the coy thing to say.

"*When* I win," he said.

We were outpacing the smoke, but when I looked back, all I could see was a fiery inferno. That nest we'd been in would be gone now. So would the market. Maybe even the creek. It was hard to care too much about a land I hated, but Scouvrel didn't seem to care either.

"Regret for the fire?" I asked him.

"Two," he said. "Some of those carvings took ages to complete."

He'd made those? I refused to be impressed.

The morning deepened as the sun rose higher, a dusty red blob in the shroud of smoke. It made me think of blood.

"Anger at your sister?" His tone was light, but he looked my way for the first time since we took off into the air and I stuck my head between the bars to try to see his expression. He was interested in the answer.

"Five."

I kept it to that. I was trying very hard not to show how delighted I was to be flying over the plains below now that we were outdistancing the fire. They glowed a pale green in my spirit vision, but there was actual light across the fields, a shadowy spirit light and it shrouded the fields of wildflowers deliciously. Ahead, the fields dipped into a large rock pit that glowed the faintest of silvers and in the pit, figures moved.

It wasn't until we were over the pit that I realized the figures were not mortal or Fae. They looked like rock come alive, vaguely man-shaped but massive. Lichen and moss grew on their striations.

"What in the world are those?"

"The silver mine?" Scouvrel asked as if it was not worth noting? "It's only operational when everyone is asleep. Usually, we wouldn't have to be bothered by it."

Bothered? A mine like that would make a town like Skundton marvelously rich. You could export those minerals down the mountains to the cities below and they would pay well for it. Everyone in Skundton would live in a fine house and wear fine clothes and decorations. They could afford to send people to the city for rare treats or to purchase books or seek schooling. The potential of such a resource made me almost ache with longing ... and to him, it was an annoyance.

"Feeling entitled?" I asked sharply.

"Five," he said lightly. "I am entitled to everything. Those are golems – raised to life by our tangled magic. You didn't think that Faeries worked, did you?"

I gaped at him. "I work. You saw me hunting and trapping. You've seen me pitch the tent and make food and hang up my clothes."

"Yes, I admire your work ethic as one admires the fruitless thrashings of a roebuck caught in a snare. Though they aid you not at all, they are all the more beautiful for their hopeless hopes."

"Work is not a hopeless hope!" I could hear the sputter in my words, and I didn't care. The arrogance!

He waved a hand dismissively. "It's for golems or servants. Not for anyone with the power to avoid it."

I couldn't seem to shut my open mouth. "Are you telling me that no Fae work at all? You just sit here while magical rocks do all your work – out of sight where you don't need to see them?"

He thought for a moment. "We create art sometimes. When we are so inclined. We decorate. We organize parties. You don't really think we … sweat. Do you?"

The horror in his eyes nearly matched the horror in my own. My mouth shut with a snap.

Hulanna had never liked work. Never done chores if she could get me to do them for her. She'd been like our mother's old expression, "one of the lilies of the field, toiling not." No wonder she loved this place. You wore pretty clothes and played games and never worked.

If I hadn't seen the Faewald with my blindfold on, I might have mistaken it for a kind of paradise. And if my father hadn't been nailed to a tree, suffering. And if the drinking establishments here weren't lined with mortal skulls. And if I wasn't in a cage.

There were a lot of "and ifs."

This place was horrible.

"Enjoyment of my home?" Scouvrel teased.

"One," I said definitively.

"Such a pity. Especially since you'll be here for the rest of your life. Which is a good reminder. I need to tell you more about our people. We are divided – always divided. The Faewald isn't so much a kingdom as it is a neverending war. Alliances form and shift. We fight with knives and words, with poison and perfectly selected apparel." He paused. "Oh. There's also magic sometimes. But magic is a tricky thing that takes more than it gives, so it's best to avoid it when you can."

"Like bargains?"

"You should be avoiding those, too, though I admit that I like bargaining with you, Little Captive. You are surprisingly easy to entrap. And now the Courts. You already know the Court of Cups where your beloved sister enjoys her reign of terror. There are also the Courts of Coins, Morning, Scales, Wings, Leaves, Knives, and Twilight."

"I'm never going to be able to keep all of them straight."

"You will. When people try to kill you, you tend to remember them."

"Promise me something, Scouvrel," I said, testily.

"I have already promised you my undying friendship and that I would never let you starve. What more could you possibly want from me?" Longsuffering patience tinted his tone. Had he really agreed to all that? The last few days had been a blur to me.

"Promise you won't sell me to someone terrible," I said.

"I cannot promise you that, Little Captive," he said after a long pause. "Because the person I intend to have purchase you is as terrible as they come."

Chapter Eleven

"Desire to sell me to my sister?" I asked, tense but playing the game.

"One."

Relief filled me, but only for a moment.

"I will do as I must, Little Captive."

"Why? Why all this secrecy and plotting? Why come to my world and drag me back here? What do you care about a prophecy and an Oolag?"

"Drag you?" His snort was all disbelief. "I could argue it was the other way around. Now, pipe down. We are navigating the Swamps of Salinger and I'd rather not be attacked by the denizens there when they come to find what is chattering in their domain."

"Fly higher," I suggested acidly.

"Excellent advice. Our enemies certainly won't be looking for a winged Fae in the sky. Especially not one with my signature smoke wings."

His tone was dry.

"Signature? I saw smoke wings on your fellows in the mortal world."

"Fellows? You mean my enemies."

"Well, you are the one who killed them, so you tell me. Maybe that's what you do with your friends. You did tell me that I'm your friend and you keep me in a cage." He wanted to sound dry? I could be drier.

"They were of my former Court. They didn't take the change in my circumstances very well."

"You don't say."

"I'd like this conversation to end, Little Nightmare."

I pulled my book from my backpack with a huff and sat in the tent, opening it up. Let's see what my ancestors had to say about the Faewald. Last time, I'd been looking for something in particular, skimming through the book for answers. This time, I started at the beginning and began to read. It started with a poem:

A wreath of writhing wraiths they were and wrath they had
a'plenty,
A twisted tawdry tangle they and called themselves the Gentry.

Hmm. Perhaps one of my ancestors had been here. That sounded very accurate to me.

Fae Year 1090

Daughters, I am writing this journal to guide you when I am gone. It has been entrusted to us to guard the people from an evil that originates in our own land. Terrible creatures that come through portals, snatching children and the sanity of men. Fear them. Fight them. And above all, do not be charmed by them. Do not love them as you love the sons of men. Do not marry them. Do not bear their children.

Good advice, though perhaps mother should have given Hulanna this book and not me. There were more warnings. I skipped ahead to the next entry.

Fae Year 1091

Funny how my ancestors were using Fae years to mark time even as they derided the Fae.

Ginnef ignored our warnings and Old Scanda had to go in the portal after her. She returned empty-handed, babbling about wraiths and a tangled world of horrors. She spoke constantly of bargains and lies. She was mad with horror. Threw herself down the well on the third day.

Cheerful histories. Tell me something I don't know, book.

Fae Year 1103

Five of us followed them into their portal. Only Janis returned. He said music keeps them at bay. Even whistling or humming has a lulling effect.

I started to hum a tune Olen was always playing.

The cage lurched, air whistling around us too quickly. We were falling. We were –

I didn't realize I'd stopped singing until we suddenly leveled off. My hand was white-knuckled where it gripped the cage and my breath was coming in fast little gasps.

"No," Scouvrel growled, like he was disciplining a puppy.

"Sorry," I muttered, returning to the book. Well. That worked.

Fire also works. They hate it. It blinds them in a way we don't truly understand. They light their way and cook their food by other means.

Interesting. The cooking was probably done by those poor shambling golems. But the lighting? How did you light something without fire?

This might also explain why Scouvrel had taken the fire so seriously. He'd refused to look at it, hadn't he?

Their magic warps time. Our people were gone a month in the Faewald, but it was only a day here. Then Tanie came back to us. The second of our people to return. She claimed to have gone through the portal an hour after Janis returned to us. For us, it was five years.

Crumbs and ashes! Twenty years could have already passed in my world. Or an hour. My mouth felt dry.

She claimed to have been kept alive speared through with a metal stake for a week. No mortal could live like that here, and yet their magic kept her alive in agony.

Like my father.

Never forget, they play with their food. Your terror feeds them. And it's fun for them to feed.

I stole a glance at Scouvrel. He was definitely enjoying his time with me. Was he feeding off *my* horror and dread? Could I use that, somehow? Hunters could work with bait. Perhaps my very fear was all the bait I needed.

Tanie tricked them into removing the stake and once it was gone, she fled. When she came through the portal, the wound was healed in the passage. She didn't think she could have survived it. And yet, somehow, the gate healed her.

So, if I could get to my father, I could free him. There was a chance despite what I'd seen.

The next dozen accounts were less informative. Women through the years who had lost loved ones and friends. Women who had fought to drive the Fae from Skundton with fire and song. Women who bound up the wounded, strapped down the insane, and fought for the lives of our town.

The last words I read as the sun faded from the sky were chilling.

We hope that by limiting this knowledge to only a few we can cleanse the memory of the Fae from our people. How else can we keep each generation from calling this evil to us again?

Well, it hadn't worked. Secrets begged to be uncovered. Making this a secret had only made it more appealing to someone like Hulanna. Poor move, ancestor ladies. Poor move.

"And now the Game intensifies. After this, I must be more circumspect with you, my lovely nightmare." Scouvrel said as he descended toward what looked like a ring of lit tents painted with garish stripes. "Ready?"

"Four." I said, trying to mean it.

Chapter Twelve

A long scream pierced the air and out of nowhere something bright pink – pinker than a wildflower in bloom – shot into the sky, screaming as it went. When it was high above us, it exploded with a *pop* and a burst of sparks. Two more bright pink screamers popped just below it.

"What was that?"

"They're firing furies off again," Scouvrel said with an annoyed voice.

"Furies?"

"They're about your size right now but with wings. You can lure them out of their dens with sweets and then light them on fire and they'll fly straight into the sky until they burn to death and then they explode."

I felt light-headed.

"They do that ... for fun?"

"I almost think you haven't been listening to me, Allie. Did I not tell you we were cruel? Did I not tell you we were worse than your wildest imaginings?"

I hadn't believed any of it. I couldn't do this.

Fuel, Allie! Use it for fuel.

"I thought your kind were afraid of fire," I said.

"Did you get that from your little book?" His laughter was barely contained.

"Yes," I said it like the word was an arrow I could shoot at him.

Now he couldn't stop the laughter. "Those little rules aren't all correct, Little Nightmare. Just because your ancestors thought a thing was true, doesn't mean it is."

"Which rules aren't true?" I asked.

"Wouldn't you like to know? Now, steel yourself. It will only get worse from here," he said, taunting me. "Terror?"

"Three." It was all I could do to keep my knees from knocking.

"See? You're not listening. That should be at least a four."

Quickly, I scrambled to pull my dried laundry from the lines, stuffing it into my pack. It made my stomach queasy to work while we moved.

Oh well. I wasn't going to lose my things to thieves or carelessness. The tent came down next, rolled carefully into the pack.

We landed on the ground in the sinking dark in the middle of the ring of tents. 'Tents' was too small of a term for these things. They were like castles made of colored silk, soaring into the sky. Vanilla and cinnamon wafted on the breeze as it ruffled my hair and the feathers of my shirt. I felt so tense that my muscles hurt with the effort of standing so rigidly.

It should have been dark, but the tents were lit with an unearthly green glow and the area between tents glowed, too. Something that buzzed was contained in jars strung from tent to tent and between them, berries hung from ribbons. The berries glowed red sand blue and purple so brightly that they put the furies to shame. White mist covered the ground, reflecting the light and making everything glow brightly with its white, slightly opaque softness. The effect was rather beautiful and dreamlike – if your dreams tended toward nightmares. It was not dark, though it was dusk. It was more like a world with the colors all wrong so that some were far too bright and others with blanched to monochrome.

Perhaps it was only my spirit vision that saw the world like this, but I didn't think so. I was starting to wonder if everyone here saw this world this way. Perhaps what was otherworldly to me was as natural as sunlight and moonbeams to them. Perhaps they lived all their lives in a projected glamor to save themselves from the horror of what this world was really like.

To remind myself, I pulled my blindfold up just long enough to see the howling, tangled darkness and hear the screams. I ripped it down immediately. Yes, the glamor was better.

Revelry had already begun, and laughter rang out from the tents along with scents that made my mouth water. Large golems, towering over Scouvrel, carved in their stone to look like perfect Fae, wove through the crowds carrying heavy-laden trays of food and drinks.

Huge bonfires were lit in between the tents, their fires – purple or blue or pure white – soaring up into the night sky.

"Illusions," Scouvrel whispered.

Fae in every shape began to emerge, dressed for parties in gowns worth more than my village. Their features were beauty made into flesh from their sparkling eyes to their berry-bright lips and flushed cheeks. Their figures were slender and whip-tight, coiled muscle and perfectly sculpted planes. I felt my cheeks go hot just looking at them. Beside them, I was worse than plain. I was almost as hideous compared to this as their real tangled forms were compared to me.

Two of them danced toward Scouvrel – complete opposites, but with twin welcoming smiles. One was tall and dark and the other short and so fair that she almost seemed translucent, their gowns made of flower petals – rose for the darker Fae and daffodil for the lighter one. They draped themselves on his arms, standing so close to him that he had trouble keeping my cage from their hands.

"Your company is a delight," he cooed to them, "but the prize in the cage belongs to me."

The one in the yellow dress laughed. I wanted to choke her.

The woman close to the nearest tent sported golden chains dripping from her ram's horns. Rubies the size of quail eggs dangled from the chains and her dress was spangled with golden loops and strings of rubies. When she smiled at Scouvrel she had a ruby in the gap between her two front teeth. Far from making her ugly, the ruby drew attention to her perfectly formed lips – made for kissing – and her perfectly curled locks of silver hair.

She didn't even seem to notice the Fae girls draped over his arms. Singing filled the air and I gasped as my eyes found a ring of women pale and gray, tied to trees with thick ropes. Where they should have had feet, there were fish tails and they sang an eerie song. I'd thought that Fae would freeze at the sound of song.

"The illusions tonight are lovely," Scouvrel whispered, leaning into the dark Fae woman's ear so that his lips touched her ear as he whispered. And yet, he clearly was saying that for my benefit. I rolled my eyes. This place fit him far too well.

"You're here, Knave of Courts!" the Fae woman with the rubies said with delight, finally joining us. "And to think, we had Balance arrive only last night! This is a delight! Your brother had hoped you would come and join us, though he is not with us tonight.

"Tell us that you've brought some diversion to the Court of Wings at Large! Do you like tonight's illusion? I thought an otherworldly circus would be best after we received your songbird missive. Why a gathering of the Court, Knave? Why a welcome extended to other Courts? Don't get me wrong, I like a good party, but I hardly had time to make it grand enough! We only brought a thousand golems with us on this expedition."

"It's a lovely party, Lady of Wings and a delightful aesthetic. I've brought a question with me," Scouvrel said with a wink. "What are the odds that you might answer it?"

"High if it comes with a kiss," she laughed and to Allie's surprise, Scouvrel kissed her cheek and then flicked her pointed ear with his finger. "A kiss and a sharp pain. You never give but you take!"

"And now I ask," he said smugly. "Why is the Court of Wings out on the plains like a common circus instead of ensconced in the fine palaces my ancestors smelted so much gold to produce?"

She leaned in close as if offering him a secret. It seemed odd with the loud shouts and revelry behind her.

"Your brother says that a Court out in the Woods is a Court that can't be overthrown by rebellion," she said. "Oh, I don't think I do like this lighting. Too harsh."

She snapped her fingers.

"Your brother is the Lord of the Court of Wings?" I asked.

"Shush, little prize," Scouvrel scolded.

Around me, the mist faded away and the light of the party changed to softened shadows and warm fuschia and orange glows, more meant for kissing in shadowed corners than for terror. The light made the Lady's coloring even lusher. If someone had told me she was the goddess of love I wouldn't have questioned them. Her dress shifted and a pair of wings unfolded at her back, decked with iridescent maroon feathers. I gasped at their sudden appearance. A single feather of such beauty would be worth a fortune at home.

"What is that thing?" the Lady asked, poking her finger through the bars at me.

"Don't touch me!" I said, but her wiggling finger smashed me into the bars.

"It talks! How delightfully grotesque!"

I drew my knife and stabbed her finger.

"Youch! It has teeth, Scouvrel!" she protested, her gorgeous voice chime-like in its beauty.

"Yes, it bites. Did I forget to warn you?" he asked smiling his most charming smile. Even I found it so stunning that I froze, entranced by the curve of his perfect mouth. "Oops."

"La, you do love a joke!" she swatted at him playfully and then looked around conspiratorially. "Watch out. The Lady of Cups arrived with the sunset and she is proclaiming high and wide that she will have your intestines for a crown by tomorrow unless you give up your little pet."

I gasped.

"Ah," Scouvrel said, sharing a wink with the Lady as she grinned at him. "But you know I am immune to threats. I plan to auction her off to the highest bidder."

"Delightful!" the Lady proclaimed. She lowered her gaze to look at me better, but wisely, stayed out of the reach of my knife. I scowled at her. "She's not very decorative though, is she? Not pretty, though you've dressed her nicely. A little wide in the hips which I understand means she can birth well, but there's no other mortals to breed her, so there won't be young."

I gasped, horrified. "Hey!"

"I'm not sure you'll get much of a price, I'm afraid, Rogue of Courts," she concluded sadly, her gorgeous face a picture of woefulness that would break the heart of royal painters. No one could paint a face so pathetically lovely.

"It's not the coin I'm after, Lady, but the entertainment," Scouvrel said wickedly.

Her grin was broad and beautiful. "Where you are, Scouvrel, there's always that!"

He danced away, whirling through the crowd of laughing Fae, so that my cage was jostled next to a man with a snake on his hat – a real snake with a mouth wider than the cage. It struck at me, barely deflected by the bars. Scouvrel snatched the cage away. The man was so beautiful that I stared, stunned by the perfection of his nutbrown skin and golden, winking eyes. The bright green snake only brought out the perfection of the perfect planes of his face.

Scouvrel spun again and I was up against a Fae woman with two tiny deer antlers poking out of her spiky white hair. She wore two living snowy owls sewn to the wide shoulder-caps of her bead-and-wood-panel gown. Their feet were wound with golden chains and tiger's eye medallions. One owl pecked at me and I yelped as its beak bit into my arm. Scouvrel smacked it gently aside and the laughing owner of the dress offered the owl a dead mouse as a treat and then we were spinning away again as I sucked on my wound.

"That hurt!"

"I told you this would hurt." No sympathy from Scouvrel.

They were all just as mad as the rest. Their clothing showing their fascination with violence and cruelty, but it was draped over bodies and faces so perfectly lovely that it was hard not to melt anytime one of them looked my way.

One Fae woman wore nothing but shimmering black panels of cloth that I could have *sworn* were attached to her body by knives plunged into her flesh. Red blood welled at their hilts and ran down the shimmering fabric, but that didn't stop her tinkling laugh or mar the perfect shine of her raven locks which hung down her back all the way to her swaying hips.

Another Fae had an elaborate updo and her long black locks were arranged artfully in curls around a green severed hand. The fingers of the hand splayed out so that it looked like it was trying to grasp the top of her skull. Her own skin was faintly green, though the effect was lovely – like a walking ripple of creek water.

I shivered at the sight of her beauty and hideousness, but I'd barely gotten over one shock when I saw the next and the next and the next.

"Delightful, isn't it? Fae society. Like a dream come alive," Scouvrel said as he worked his way toward a raised dais. I did not think the word 'delightful' applied.

Just in front of the dais, I caught a glance of my sister, her head thrown back in laughter. She was wearing a dress made entirely of white pearls and nothing else. Beside her, her Fae lover – Lord Cavariel – sparkled like a living moonbeam, his perfect features awash in silver light that came from within him so beautiful that it broke my heart – an angel come alive. The glances he shot at those around them were sharp and deadly, though. As if a sword had come to life and walked among people.

My sister, I realized, had pointed ears now and her perfection was equal to the Fae around her. Was it possible to ... become Fae? And had she become one of them?

I tried to catch her eye without success. Was there anything of the mortal girl I'd known left in there? Any compassion? Any touch of mortality?

Scouvrel saw what I was looking at and his chuckle was pure cruelty.

"Your sister will live forever now. Isn't that nice? Immortality without moral obligations."

"You can *become* Fae?" I asked with a gasp.

"Under some circumstances. Tell me, Little Hunter. Desire for immortality?"

"One," I said firmly.

"Good," he replied. "Your life is like the flight of an arrow, fast and deadly. I don't dare miss a moment of it."

Really? That was how he saw me? He looked at me and in the middle of this strange place that didn't seem real, that look did seem real. It seared painfully across my soul and for a moment I thought I detected pity.

"The game only gets tougher from here," Scouvrel confessed, looking guilty for a half of a second – so briefly that I almost didn't believe my eyes.

"Difficulty?" I asked.

"Five," he said with a mischievous grin. "Almost, I am afraid to mount that dais."

"Be a man," I said, boldly, pretending I didn't feel an urgent need for a trip to the outhouse.

"I am no man," he hissed, darkness seeming to fill his eyes. "I am Faerie through and through."

"You can still try," I said, feigning a boldness I did not have myself.

"I am male, is that not enough?" he asked.

"Not hardly," I replied.

"Then I shall try to play the man, if that is what pleases you, Little Nightmare."

He strode up the dais, stood tall and lifted my cage high in the air.

"The Knave of Courts is here," he proclaimed, sweeping an elegant bow to the crowd. Cheers erupted and Scouvrel basked in them, waiting until the applause quieted before taking a seat on a carved throne and holding the cage out for them to see with a single forefinger. "You've heard that I've caught an interesting little curiosity. You've heard correctly. Some of you have attempted to take her from me by force, but rest assured, I have repulsed all efforts to end our fun. By the Law of Games, I announce a new revelry for you all!"

There was a delighted gasp as every Fae around set down glasses and foods to crowd around, their eyes showing their utter delight at Scouvrel. He hadn't lied. They loved a game. Apparently, there were even rules about them.

"As you are well aware," he said, throwing a leg over the arm of the seat dramatically and setting my cage beside it on the wooden arm. "The Law of Games states a game may not be interrupted without a head tax being paid." He wagged a finger at the crowd. "So, stop trying to end the fun prematurely!" That got him a delighted chuckle. "And, to top that, the game may not end, or the prize be awarded until the full terms of the game are complete. Come and play with me, my loves! This game is an auction of wealth and blood and magic. All bids for this curiosity will be entertained and the highest bid shall win as determined by the Face of Ages standard on the exchange of blood, magic and souls!" None of that sounded good.

"Bidding on my Nightmare begins NOW." He lifted a hand and then chopped it down violently. "I will take all bids and the highest bidder will possess her, body and soul."

I felt my heart sinking down, down, down into the depths of my belly.

Chapter Thirteen

When we were children, everyone was always waiting for Hulanna for the party to start. Things just weren't the same when she wasn't there with her quick teasing and her bright smile. That hadn't changed in the Faewald. I bounced nervously from foot to foot as she swept up onto the dais, her pearl dress rippling as she moved. Her feet were bare. That struck me as odd. Who walked around without shoes? What if you had to run?

There was way too much I didn't know about this world.

"Hulanna. You little traitor," I practically spat. "Where is our father?"

She ignored me, stepping up so close to Scouvrel's chair that all I could see of her was her waist. She wasn't wearing anything under those pearls! Our mother would be horrified.

One of the Fae women who had been hanging from Scouvrel's arm slid up to drape herself over the other arm of his chair. She winked at me through kohl-lined eyes and I scowled. What business did she have to look so decorative? She should have a little more respect for herself. Women were more than decorations. Decorations could be replaced.

"You'd better have taken him down from those spikes, sister," I growled, ignoring the decoration-girl. "Or I will drag you home and switch you until you can't sit for a week."

Her hand shot out and knocked my cage aside and I gritted my teeth, gasping as it tipped over and fell. My feet knocked out from under me and I hit the bars hard, gasping as my breath was stolen by the impact. Ungh! I was braced for impact, but something snatched the falling cage out of the air, righting it gently enough that I merely slid to the floor. My ribs ached. Were they bruised? It hurt to sit up and check. What had happened to my sister to steal away all her pity?

Or had she always had the seed of this within her?

The cage was slammed back up on the arm of the wooden throne and my teeth clashed together. The decorative Fae girl giggled delightedly like this was a fun game. She slid up the side of the chair and whispered something in Scouvrel's ear that made him laugh with her.

"You don't have the right to auction off my sister, Knave of Courts," Hulanna challenged. I shoved my head between the bars, twisting to look up at her giant face. She'd outlined her eyes with dark kohl. Rather than making her look seductive like decoration-girl, It made her look menacing. "She belongs to me."

And yet she wasn't addressing me, or even looking at me. Nice, sister. Maybe she wanted to nail me to a tree, too. A matched set with dear old Dad.

"Oh, I don't think so, Lady of Cups," Scouvrel said. His smile was smooth, and he stayed in his relaxed position on the oak chair as if nothing could shake him. His smoke wings had disappeared and his shirt had fallen open almost to his belly button, revealing creeping tattoos across his chest and belly. I recognized the feathers and the mouse skull, but the thorns ... had those been there yesterday? I didn't recognize them. The tattoo thorns – like the dark green ones winding around my forearms – were threaded through the feathers.

I pushed up my sleeve and frowned. Was that a feather in my woven thorns? Strange. You couldn't trust anything in this place.

"I am the one who took this Captive. By rights of Claim, she is mine to sell as I wish."

"And I wish to bid," a harsh voice said, slightly slurred.

I craned my neck to look past my sister.

A tall Fae man, almost as wide as he was tall stood behind her. I'd never seen anything like him. I swallowed at his sheer size. His eyes were very dark, framed with thick brows and his ears were properly pointed, his hair cut close to his head. So far, so Fae. But what about the greenish tinge to his skin? It was darker than it would be if he were merely ill. And what about the lower canines sticking out of his lower lip? No wonder he was having trouble speaking clearly. A sword was slung across his back and he wore a shirt of pale leather that wasn't stitched from any animal I'd ever known. Someone had embroidered a white fox on the front of it, crying three bloody tears.

How pleasant.

On instinct, I drew up my blindfold and shuddered. He was twisted like all the rest – but sharp blades peeked in and out of his tangled flesh. I pulled the blindfold back down, shuddering.

He leered at me and I scowled back.

"But I was the one who sent you to the mortal world, Knave," Hulanna said, stepping back to where I could see her face again, her cheeks flushed. It was strange to see her looking like a giant above me. Her auburn hair glowed beautifully in the low light, threaded with more pink-tinted pearls. They were

the size of my fist. "You were my prisoner. We had an agreement."

The pretty fae girl began to kiss Scouvrel's neck just as if
we weren't all there watching. I wanted to cut her pointed ears
off with my knife. Not because I was jealous. And not because
it looked more than indecent to do that in public – though if
she'd lived in Skundton the women of the town would have
locked her in a storeroom until she married any man she did
that with in public. I just didn't like that she was distracting
him when he was taking bids for my fate. That was all. I certainly wasn't jealous.

"Yes, the bargain was, 'I will let you out of this prison if you
go to the mortal world and find my sister. You may not give
your loyalty to any other until you return to the Faewald or offer her to any other Fae.'" His smile was wicked and my sister
paled as she saw the flaw in her bargain. "I found your sister.
I kept my loyalty to myself until I returned to our world. And
look, I offer her to no one. I have merely put her up for auction
– for sale. That's not an offer. It's a sale."

Hulanna spat. It seemed horribly crude for something as
gorgeously refined as she was. I ducked back into the cage. Any
spatter would soak me.

"And I am ready to bid – generously," the green Fae said. "I
will start the bidding with the offer of the Tower of Heights.
Complete with the golems that serve there."

There was a gasp from the audience around us.

Scouvrel's mouth turned up in the corners but he lifted his
chin arrogantly. He seemed younger like this. As if he was some
prince so far down the line that he couldn't inherit the throne
but still had the power to burn and destroy at will.

"The Knave recognizes the bid of the Court of Twilight. Any winning bid will have to be of greater value."

Hulanna's face flushed. "But that's worth a fortune!"

She still wasn't looking at me. Still didn't care that I was her blood and I was locked in a cage. What had become of her? What would the women of Skundton do with someone like her?

I reached for my blindfold and Scouvrel caught my eye, shaking his head almost imperceptibly. But I needed to see. I needed to know.

I pulled up my blindfold anyway, biting my tongue and tasting blood at the sight of Hulanna. She was tangled, just like him. A living wraith, ever twisting, ever raging, no longer mortal at all.

I swallowed down the blood and pulled down my blindfold. Scouvrel rolled his eyes at me.

And that's how it was. I'd had a sister. A sister I'd loved. And now I didn't.

What would make her choose this? Could it have been against her will?

"I'll entertain your bid of course," Scouvrel said, tapping his long fingers on the arm of the chair.

"We stand with the Court of Cups," a man said from behind Hulanna, stepping up to her side. He was the most plainly dressed of anyone there, though a long, scaled tail snaked out of his trousers. "We will back their interests in this matter."

"Of course, you do," Scouvrel said, sounding bored. "Coins always stands with Cups. Do either of you have a bid, or are you wasting my time?"

"We can't trust you to take the bids fairly," Hulanna said, as if playing a trump card. "You are known for your cheating and lying ways."

Scouvrel laughed. "I see Balance lurking in the back. Let him take the bids and write them down in his little book and he shall declare the winner. Whoever is willing to bid highest, before the end of seven days, gets the captive. The Court of Twilight has already placed a strong starting bid. "

There was a rustle of bodies in the crowd and I struggled to see through them. Something was moving, forcing the crowd to part. The small noises of irritation suggested he hadn't taken the simplest route.

He emerged from the press of bodies, mounting the dais and forcing Hulanna to the side. One side of his head had black hair and the other half, white, though both sides were slicked back with something that gleamed maroon in the light. That had better not be blood.

He was winged – one white feathered wing, one dark bat-like wing were on opposite sides to the colors of his hair. His clothing was also a tangle of black and white fluttering patches and a small brass scale hung from a delicate chain around his neck.

"You called?" he asked, quirking his dark eyebrow.

"I offer you the role of Game Master, Balance of Courts," Scouvrel said. So, this was one of the other four who had roles outside the Fae Courts. I'd met the Sooth. The Knave. The Balance. I hoped I'd never meet the one called Kinslayer. "And I bid you all goodnight. I tire of these roiling emotions. None of them tastes at all sharp and you know how I loathe dullness. Do better next time, fellow Fae."

"Where are you going, Rogue?" Hulanna demanded.

"Planning on sending more assassins after me, lovely Lady?" Scouvrel almost spat the words.

"I wouldn't violate the Law of Games," she said, raising her chin.

"I won't tempt you to do otherwise," he said, snatching up my cage, shaking off his admirers and shooting into the sky like a black star with a final reminder, "Place your bids, everyone!"

Chapter Fourteen

I clung to the bars, my heart in my throat as we plunged toward the night sky, the circus tents below us fading away.

"Dramatic much?" I asked, but my words were fainter than I wished they were.

"Gossip is our friend in this. And for this to work, I need it to fester without me there."

"You're not really going to sell me to that green monster?"

"The Orc? He's a representative of the Court of Twilight. And yes, if no one outbids him, he will have you."

"I hate you, Scouvrel," I said, frustration welling up inside me. There was no escape. There was no way out.

"That's the spirit!"

"What makes your people think they can buy and sell mortals?"

"Long experience. But I'll tell you what, I'll let you out of the cage for a while to stretch your legs, how does that sound?"

"It sounds like you want something."

We dipped down, soaring toward the sea. I gasped as the wind whipped through the cage and he swept up to a lonely, dark tree clutching the side of the cliff above the sea. Brine mixed with the scent of grass and growing things and a lingering scent that I was starting to think of as Scouvrel – cloves and cinnamon and something animal underneath.

"I want only one of your rare kisses," he said, laughing.

"I think the Fae girls back there would have given you all the kisses you could have wanted," I said dryly as he landed beside the tree and places his hand on the trunk almost affectionately. "More than kisses, if their sultry looks were speaking for them."

"I'm sure they would," Scouvrel said with a wicked glint in his eye.

I frowned. He'd said that with his same evil, teasing tone just like always. And yet ... and yet there was something off about it. Something that made me ask, "Scouvrel, before you met me ..." I didn't know how to say it and it hung in the air. "I mean, you've lived a long time ... hadn't you ever ... married?"

"Before I met you?" He snorted, raising the cage so he could look in my eyes. He watched me as long seconds ticked away and I thought he wasn't going to answer me until suddenly he shook his head and winked at me.

"No, Little Nightmare. In all the many years before you first terrified me, I never ... married." He raised an eyebrow as if to suggest more by the word. "That kind of knowledge of a person has its own kind of power. I have never felt so overcome that I have desired another person to know what makes me gasp with delight or sigh with pleasure. Knowledge is power. And I have kept that power to myself." He looked up at the stars before continuing. "It's so much harder to be cruel when you're in love. And so much easier to be betrayed."

What did you say to that? My brow was still furrowed when he walked behind the tree into a dip in the ground between the tree and a large boulder. The dip sank into the earth with a suddenness that surprised me. From what I could tell, it became a tunnel or an entrance into a place under the roots of the tree.

Scouvrel paused. "I know that you want to escape, Little Hunter. I know that you want to go and free your father. But what you really *need* right now is to be my ally."

"And what do you get out of that," I whispered back. For some reason, speaking aloud felt wrong right now.

"I don't want to say."

"Then why would I be your ally?" I hissed.

He looked torn, pacing in a circle before flinging himself against the dirt wall beside the dip and holding the cage in both hands to observe me.

"If I tell you … if … I want your pledge of loyalty."

I scowled. "I won't agree to pledge loyalty to you without knowing what you're trying to do. I could be committing my-self to anything!"

He rubbed his face with his hand. He looked tired. And knee-tremblingly gorgeous. His cruel lips parted slightly as he regarded me. He licked them nervously with a deliciously pink tongue.

"I'll tell you my reasons. And then, if you feel they are enough, you can give me your pledge, free and of your own will."

"I want to save my father. Anything that goes against that will make it impossible to pledge anything. Besides, why should I pledge to something when you've pledged to noth-ing!"

"Nothing? I gave you my pledge of undying loyalty!"

"As a joke!"

"Trust me, it was no joke." His eyes lit with passion.

I leaned in close, my head stuck through the bars.

"Then tell me."

I was so focused on him, that I didn't see or hear anything else.

"I – " he started to say. Out of the darkness, something shot out and hit his head.

The cage fell from his hand I gripped the bars, screaming. It hit the ground and my shoulder and back hit with it. Pain flared through me, leaving me gasping against the bars of the cage. Someone lifted the cage and righted it. I slid down the bars to the floor, panting and gasping for breath as my hands fisted in pain. Stars danced across my vision and agony flared brightly in my head.

What in the world –

Red teardrops marred a white embroidered fox.

The cage lifted further.

A single black eye, wreathed in green skin, regarded me with cool indifference.

"Got you," the orc growled. "He really needs to learn to hide his safe houses better. But it wouldn't be much of a game if he didn't slip up sometimes, would it?"

I gasped as the cage rocked wildly, renewing the pain in my shoulder and back. I thought I might pass out. I tried to focus on what was happening.

The orc had me.

He angled toward a huge creature – huge even compared to him, never mind me. It stood low to the ground – glowing a copper color – and it was covered from nose to tail in overlapping scales. Someone had taken some time to set a saddle on the creature as well as a bridle.

My heart sped up, my hands trembling as I struggled to sit. I hurt from top to bottom.

"Pangolin. Kneel," the orc ordered, and the creature lowered itself to the ground as the orc mounted. All I saw was glowing scales and a green arm holding my cage up.

"You can't just take me like this," I protested. "I'm being auctioned to the highest bidder."

He said nothing, but I heard rustling above the cage and then it was swaying from an anchor point on the saddle.

"You aren't allowed to interrupt a game!" I called.

"Who says it's interrupted, mortal? I'm merely modifying it."

I began to hum, trying to stun him but he shook the cage violently, and I smacked the bars, hitting my injured shoulder a second time, only to be flung immediately in the other direction. My face smashed against the bars, I tasted blood, and then I slipped to the floor, darkness closing in around my vision.

"Please," I begged.

"Yes, beg. I love the taste of your fear. It is sharp and invigorating. I feel fifty years younger," the orc said.

I tried to speak again, but the blackness stole my words away.

BOOK TWO

A curse on all your tangled heads,
A curse to bind, a curse to rend,
To keep you in this magic cage,
To bind you up and hem your rage,
To mute your wrath and hold your bite,
And hobble you before the fight.
A curse to save, a curse to kill,
A curse to thieve, a curse to fill.
- Tales of the Faewald

Chapter Fifteen

I woke to the jostle of the cage shaking me back and forth. Nausea overwhelmed me with a wave of panic. Gasping for breath, I crawled to the edge of the cage, stuck my head out of the bars and vomited.

Harsh laughter greeted me.

"As long as you're sick, we won't waste food on you. Get it out of your system, wingless fury."

"I'm not a fury," I gasped, wiping my mouth. It was all I could do to stay on my knees as the movement of the bronze-scaled creature rocked the cage back and forth. It hit the black-leather-clad leg of the orc with every swing, jostling the cage in a stomach-twisting jolt.

My head pounded like a drum, knives of pain shooting into my mind with every jolt. My shoulder joined the symphony of pain, followed by my ribs. Great. I was a mess.

Was the orc planning on killing me? It would be so easy when I was trapped in this cage. You could throw it in water, or from a height, or simply refuse to feed me. But he hadn't killed me yet and he'd had time to do it.

I shuddered. I'd never feared this with Scouvrel, despite all his claims of cruelty and brutality. And he *had* been cruel and brutal. He would have sold me to this orc if the orc hadn't stolen me. And yet ... somehow this felt different. I felt vulnerable in a way I never had before.

I wedged myself against the side of the cage that looked out across the land, taking in the rustling grass alive with furies and pixies. Their tiny forms – no bigger than mine – lit the world with colorful sparks. The scent of timothy grass and sea salt wafted over me, clearing my head and helping me to think.

It's no different, Allie. It's no different than before. You're still a prisoner. Your best bet is still to gather information and try to escape. These people don't know how to put you in the cage, which means that if you can get out, you can really be free.

Except Scouvrel had the key.

Despair washed over me and I gritted my teeth against the blackness. No, Allie. There was no room for despair. There was only room to fight. If I gave up now, no one would save my father. No one would destroy the Faewald and keep my people safe. I didn't dare be weak. I had to be strong as nails. I had to find the iron in my core and burn this world to the ground with it.

I gritted my teeth and pulled myself to my feet.

Across my vision, another giant pangolin rode past carrying a female orc Fae. Her dark hair streamed out behind her, the pale skull painted over her face failing to disguise her full lips and wide smirk. She glanced my way before riding past.

"Don't lose the trinket, Ghadrot," she growled at the orc above me. "We made a terrible enemy by snatching it up."

Ghadrot growled an intangible response.

I was getting information. I knew the orc was called Ghadrot. That was good, right? And they'd made an enemy by taking me – though I wasn't sure who that was. Hulanna, perhaps?

I took my time and watched them. There were maybe a dozen. All orc Fae. They seemed to favor modest, war-like clothing made of leather and heavily embroidered with sigils. They favored gold rings in their ears, some of them bearing at least a dozen. They seemed to indicate rank. Those with more earrings mocked those with fewer. It didn't go the other way.

They rode for hours without stopping for a break. No one complained. No one growled about the ride. Each orc was studded with bronze weapons. Axes. Huge swords with chips missing in the blades. Knives curved, knives straight, knives that curved around the knuckles like a half-moon. Staves and halberds. Gauntlets that looked like they'd been cut from pangolin scales.

Almost, I liked this kind of Fae better than the other. They were beautiful, but not nearly as pretty as the rest. They were muscled, orderly, and their eyes were sharp. They made me think of myself. If I was fae, I would be one of these orc-fae.

Perhaps, I could strike a deal with them.

We did not stop to rest until dawn was nearly upon us. They pitched a camp in a forest glen with the efficiency I imagined trained soldiers would have. The orc handling me set my cage down near the cookpots and shoved a bloody scrap of meat through the bars like I was a prized pet.

"What kind of meat is it?" I asked, but he only grunted.

I regarded it for a long time as the orcs cooked their dinner – more meat scalded over the open fire with tea and what smelled like a malt drink of some kind.

I was not hungry enough to eat uncooked red meat of unknown origin, though I poked at it with a finger. Perhaps it would seem more appealing tomorrow. But I doubted that.

I set up my tent with care, spreading my blanket inside. The long days and nights without proper sleep were catching up with me. I left the door of the tent open so that I could see what was going on in the camp.

Before they went to their bedrolls, the orcs dumped their used pots and pans and dishes beside my cage. It was all just junk they had to carry around, I supposed.

What they didn't notice was that they'd left one of their knives close enough to the bars that I could reach it.

I waited hours until the last of them had drifted into snores and the Fae woman on watch had drifted to the perimeter of the camp and then I reached out the bars and slid the knife inside my cage. It was too big to wield easily. I certainly couldn't stab anything with it, but it was solid metal. And it was long. With great care, I set it between the bars and set to work trying to lever them apart. I couldn't squeeze between the bars, but my head could, which meant it wouldn't take much for the rest of me to make the squeeze.

Who wouldn't try to escape a group of bloodthirsty kidnappers who wore jackets sewn of mortal skin?

I knew I'd been at it for several hours when I heard the guard change. No one stopped to check on me.

It didn't matter. By the time the sun began to set, and my orc kidnapper had awoken, I hadn't moved the bars enough to get free. I was leaning on the knife, exhausted, shoulder aching, tears of frustration streaking my face, when he found me there.

With a laugh, he extracted the knife but though his voice was deep and raspy, his words were not unkind.

"Still have a little spirit, do you, insect? The Court of Twilight likes spirit. It makes you more fun to break."

His words were still ringing in my mind when he tied me back to the saddle. I crept into the tent and fell asleep on my blankets but my dreams were full of nightmares of insects trying to escape a honey trap.

When next I woke, I was damp.

Surf sprayed across the cage from where it was lashed to the seat of a boat.

"Pull! Pull! Pull!" A voice bellowed as the boat lurched and rocked over roiling waves under a dark sky.

I stood up in my cage.

"There's a leak in the boat!" Someone growled. "Bail, golems, bail!"

I couldn't see the action. Huge stone bodies blocked out the sight of what was going on. But the golems worked silently, and the grunts and growls were all orcs.

"If the Court of Cups wants our help, they should provide boats that aren't sinking," a voice sneered.

Squeaking filled my ears.

"Even the rats agree!"

Rats! My eyes widened. At this size, a rat would be like a bear to me. Desperately, I reached into my pack and drew out my bow and quiver. I slung the quiver over my shoulder, stringing the bow in a single motion.

The pack! It slammed against the bars, the top opening at the impact. I hurried to it, stumbling to my knees and crawling the last half of the distance. I closed up the top of the pack, tying it to the bars.

My tent had collapsed, a mess now. Only one rope was still tied to a bar and the fabric of the tent was tangled with the blanket. I tried to kick it to the side, but already, rats swarmed around my cage, squeaking, and squealing. My stomach flipped as one of them slid between the cage bars with ease, rearing up in front of me.

With my spirit vision, he was all brilliant red streaks and shadow, not so much a rat as the feeling of a rat – a living squeak.

I drew an arrow and fired as fast as I could. The rat slammed its forelegs down as I loosed again. It was too large. With my arrows so small, I didn't have enough stopping power. It was like fighting a grizzly bear with a bow.

I dodged to the side just in time to avoid a snarling attack. Again.

I snatched another arrow from my quiver, picking my spot. The arrow slid through the rat's chest with ease, clattering against a bar on the other side.

The rat reared again and then froze, falling against the bars.

Around us, more rats ran squealing from the rising water.

Steeling my jaw, I collected my arrows, wiping them clean on the rat's fur.

Rats poured around my cage, but one look at their brother, dead on the floor of my cage, and they chose to go around it.

I was still the Hunter. I could still bring down my prey. I stood over the rat, thinking about that. I wasn't some shrieking girl they'd kidnapped. I wasn't going to sit in the corner and give up. I needed to show these Fae what kind of person I was, just like I'd shown Scouvrel. I'd earned his respect. Sort of. I could earn theirs.

"The threat of strength saves you from having to use it," my father had told me one afternoon when I was fourteen. He'd had his quiver full of arrows and a bow on his back, three knives strapped to his belt and a thick staff in his hand. He adjusted the quiver on my back. "Strap on every knife you have."

I'd done exactly that.

When we joined the other able-bodied fighters of the village outside the graveyard, everyone had been armed just like us.

And when we marched on the graveyard, the three men raiding it had fled after a single look at us. It had taken all day to rebury the dead. Not that I'd minded. I could work all day without feeling worn. And the dead deserved respect.

"We could have scared them off on our own," I'd said to my father on our way home. "We didn't need the other townsfolk or all those weapons. You could have shot them all."

"Sometimes you don't need to kill if you can make them think it's not worth dying over. All of us together, well, we prevented death like that. Always choose life when you can, Allie."

So, here I was in a Fae ship on the rolling waves with squealing rats around me and a dead one still warm in my cage. Maybe I could show a threat to these orcs. Maybe it could prevent deaths later.

Chapter Sixteen

By the time the boat was pulling into shore, I had the rat skinned and his skin scraped and stretched over the back bars of the cage. If they kept me in here for much longer, I might be grateful for the fur as disgusting as rat fur was. It was large enough that it could cover me completely, like a huge bear-hide cloak. Maybe I should get used to the idea. Allie Hunter, hunter of rats.

A huge black eye filled one side of the cage as my orc captor looked inside. I was tossing the last of the rat's carcass out of the cage along with what was left of the rotting meat he'd given me to eat.

"It's a shame we have to give you to the Court of Cups, fury. You'd fit in perfectly with the Court of Twilight."

"Then don't give me away," I said boldly. "Keep me around. I can help you with your rat problem."

His laughter was joined by some of the others around him. Beneath me, the cage shook as the boat reached the shore.

"Ah, but then we won't have a Feast for Ravens and I've been longing for one for years now." His eyes half-closed in anticipated pleasure.

"What's a Feast for Ravens?" I asked as he lifted the cage up. He seemed to be in a talkative mood. Let him talk. Let's see what I could learn.

"War, fury. Ravens are carrion eaters."

"Then why not call it a Feast for Turkey Vultures or A Feast for Skunks," I said. "They eat carrion, too."

He snorted. "See? I would like your company. Almost as much as I will like bathing in the blood of my enemies."

"Which enemies?"

He shrugged. "Doesn't matter, really. I'll happily kill any of them."

"The Court of Wings, perhaps?" I pressed.

He shrugged. "Hopefully, we'll provoke a better Court than that. Wings is already out in the fields avoiding the displeasure of the people and hoping their guts aren't spilled across their floors like the Court of Knives. They don't want to see their Court laid waste, so they play picnic all night in the woods. We don't play children's games in the Court of Twilight. We play the kind of games that get you killed. We play them bold and bright and honest. And we don't pretend to be your friend when we aren't."

So, that meant that Scouvrel's former Court and the Court of Twilight were enemies. And Twilight was going to sell me to Cups. Which I did not want.

"Where was the ruler of the Court of Wings? I asked. "I didn't see him."

The orc laughed. "See? And you have a sharp eye to boot. If you weren't so small and if you weren't the price for a good war, we could make something interesting of you."

"I'm Allie Hunter," I said boldly.

"They call me Ghadrot Worm-Eater."

"And did you have to eat a lot of worms to get that name?"

"It's a proclamation of my greatness. When you die, you're food for the worms. The worms should watch out because if I ever die, they will be food for me."

"I'm sure they're terrified to hear it."

We'd been following the other orcs along a path that wound between towering moss-encrusted rocks and up a long slope. When we reached the top, a golden light spilled from a huge barrow cut into the hill. Smoke curled in a dozen pillars through the tufted roof of the barrow. We passed a pair of orcs turning a massive spit with a beast I didn't recognize close to fully roasted, its juices spitting and squealing as it cooked. Another pair we passed were skinning something that looked disturbingly like the giant pangolin we'd ridden. I hoped that wasn't on the menu.

Smaller barrows held what looked like homes cut into the hillsides and rocks. Orcs of varying sizes and with varying levels of rings in their ears stood in pairs or clusters, tussled in the long grass, or sharpened swords, or drank from frothing mugs. There was chanting and laughter and the kind of guffawing I usually associated with boys my age. Male or female, they all were marked by scars, tattoos, and rippling muscles.

I had to admit that Ghadrot was right. I would have loved to be a part of this Court, war and all.

A huge orc stood at the sight of our party, long braids hanging down his shoulder and a grim expression on his face.

"Ghadrot Worm Eater," he said, his eyes narrowing. "Back from the sea."

"Feast-leader Werex," Ghadrot said, fist pounding his chest so hard that it made my cage tremble. I bit back a curse and grabbed the bars of the cage. "I bring the token of our intent. Captured without bloodshed as you requested."

"Excellent," Werex said. Around him, other orcs stood up. They looked almost like a village council. One of them, a woman, had lines on her face. How old did a Fae have to get to have lines on her face? And the others bore so many scars that it was hard to imagine what they would have looked like when they were young. "You will be rewarded with the first strike when the Feast arrives."

I risked a glance up to Ghadrot and nearly flinched at the bloodthirsty eagerness in his eyes.

On second thought, maybe I wouldn't fit in here.

"Bring the token to me."

Ghadrot hurried forward, stiffening in a salute when he was a pace away from Werex.

Werex plucked me from his hand. Beside him, a woman in a heavy hooded cloak emerged from the shadows to stand beside him. Her antlers stuck out from the hood.

The Sooth. She was playing both sides. Or maybe no side. Scouvrel had said she was one of the four who didn't have a Court.

"It's small," Werex said, frowning at me.

"Handy with that little bow, though," Ghadrot said with a toothy grin. "Killed a nice rat with it. If she wasn't key to starting the Feast, I'd almost be tempted to feed her scraps and see what she does. Her emotions are ... sharp."

Werex inhaled. "Tasty."

I shivered. I was tasty? To orcs? Stars preserve me!

"I like what you've done with your Court," I said, looking around.

Werex laughed, but his laughter was not friendly like Ghadrot's had been. Furtively, I looked for my kidnapper, but he had disappeared already into the throngs of Fae.

"This is not my Court. This is only an encampment on the shores of the Sea of Tears. This is an afterthought. A temporality. An illusion." His lower jaw seemed to jut more than other orcs as his brows knit together.

"Then I look forward to seeing your true Court." I tried to keep my voice steady, but there was something about this place that was making my heart race. My hand twitched toward my blindfold, longing to go back home and see the normal forest around me, lonely and friendly. To see the trails of familiar animals, the smell of familiar trees, maybe even hear Olen's mandolin playing across the fields. It was good that he'd lost faith in me. Good that he hadn't come. If he had, he'd be trapped, too. Or worse.

"Where are you, Court of Cups?" Werex growled, his voice so loud that it left a ringing in my ears.

My sister. Here.

I swallowed, feeling my eyes sting from going so wide and my knees weaken.

I turned in the cage.

But it wasn't my sister who appeared. The High Lord Cavariel stepped out from a nearby barrow, his perfect features curving into a smile. He smelled of rare perfumes and secrets.

Werex grunted at him. "We promised you the other half, Cups. And here she is."

The other half. Other half of whatever it was my sister and I were supposed to be. I felt my breath hitch. I didn't like the glint in Cavariel's eye as he snatched up the cage. His clothing was more civilized than the Court of Twilight was. Perfectly cut and brocaded in gold, his coat collar brushed his jaw. Foamy lace spilled from the collar of his open shirt and the cuffs of his rich sleeves. Maroon velvet leggings dipped into high tooled-leather boots as his dragonfly wings fluttered in the breeze. He looked exactly like the Prince of Faerie I had thought him to be when we first met.

But I had learned that the Faewald was no heaven of perfect delights.

I didn't think that my heart could beat faster, but it was. Whatever I feared from my sister, I feared more from Cavariel.

Cavariel lifted the cage, his cold eye inspecting me.

"Wine," he said. "As much of it as you can carry."

"I can't carry much when I'm this size," I said, putting a hand arrogantly on my hip.

He sneered and turned his gaze to Werex to indicate who he really was addressing. Had my sister really married this perfectly horrible creature?

"First you want the caged fury and now you want to be drunk? When do the games end?" Werex spat. "Where is the Feast of Ravens you promised us?"

Cavariel hissed and the orc's eyes narrowed. They weren't going to fight right here, were they? They'd better not! One misplaced foot could squash the life out of me.

"Just bring the wine," Cavariel said. He held Werex's gaze until a thump sounded nearby. The sound of wood cracking split the air. When he finally turned to look, swinging my cage as he moved, two orcs had brought a cask of wine and opened it with a crowbar.

"Enough for you?" Werex asked, a hidden threat in his throat. "Have a care or your Court may well follow the Court of Leaves. Would your people enjoy a millennia in the Tower of Escape? We've sided with you for this Feast, but we could just as easily side with another."

Cavariel leaned in toward Werex and I was surprised by the malice in his face. The snowy lace of his cuff obscured my view – and I was grateful. I didn't want to be part of this fight. Neither participant really wanted me alive beyond what they could use me for.

It worried me that I was in his hand. I'd been afraid of my sister since the moment I saw my father held suspended in the tortures she'd prepared for him. I'd never considered that her husband might be the true madman. But the glimmer in his eye was not the glimmer of sanity.

"Don't threaten me ... orc. Bow before your better."

The orc seized him by the throat, shaking him, but Cavariel laughed as he shook. "I have spies in your court, Werex. Spies and assassins. Crush my throat and they will crush your skull. And the skulls of your young and your ladies. I've given them all the orders they need."

Werex's nostrils flared, his lip twitching, but he released Cavariel and I sighed with relief. No matter who won, I was certain I would lose.

"Watch this," Cavariel said, laughing as if it had all been a huge joke. He really was insane.

He moved so quickly that I didn't have time to react – barely had time to suck in a breath before he plunged my cage into the barrel.

Chapter Seventeen

When we were fifteen, Hulanna stumbled home drunk and I found my mother crying behind the house the next day.

"What's wrong?" I asked her, appalled. Had something worse happened?

"Oh Allie, I'm worried about your sister," she said. "She hates it here. She hates it so much. And now she and her friends are drinking near the stone circle."

"I think you're taking this too hard," I'd said gently. "Our friends drink sometimes. It's ... it's just something they do."

I didn't even know where they got it from. No one ever told me about those impromptu parties until afterward.

"You don't understand," my mother said, her face pale. "Skundton is a place on the edge of another world. We can't afford to let our guard down. Not ever. None of us can. Especially not there."

She was kidding, right? We lived on the edge of nowhere. If you wanted real excitement you had to travel for weeks to Queen Anabetha's court and fight for a place with the knights. You'd never find excitement here.

"Especially not where?"

"Promise me that you won't go up there with them, Allie," my mother said desperately. "Promise me!"

"Sure," I'd said because I really didn't care. Hunting was a lot more interesting than whatever Hulanna's friends were doing. My mother was just getting herself upset over nothing.

I didn't hear about any other parties after that. Which didn't mean there weren't any, only that no one had bothered to tell Allie Hunter.

Chapter Eighteen

My nose filled with wine and I tried to force it out without losing too much air.

I swam to the top of the cage, but it was fully submerged and though I battered at the top of the cage, there was no give at all.

My lungs burned.

Panic filled me, screaming through my mind like a demon rising from hell.

I thrashed madly against the roof of the cage, even though I knew there was no way out. I couldn't just give in. The iron was impervious to my blows.

I was helpless.

For the first time in my life, I felt pure fear. A spike of madness that stole all reason, stole all hope, stole everything away until there was only me – vulnerable and shaking. Dying.

This was where I would die. In a barrel of wine. Only in the Faewald would someone drown you in wine for no reason. I would have sobbed if I could spare the air.

My whole body tugged away from the roof in a sudden surge of movement.

And then suddenly I was in the air again, wine draining all around me. I fell to the floor of the cage, coughing, red wine spewing from my lungs. They hurt so much. Tears leaked from my eyes, mixing in the wine. Tears of terror and relief rolled together. Relief that I could breathe. Terror that he might do it again.

I sucked down another breath, and before I could scream, I was plunged under the wine again.

Terror made my thoughts jagged and distorted. And with them, my sense of time. My sense of self. My sense of anything. My eyes swelled wide, searching in the burgundy depths for any salvation.

And then there was air, leaving me clinging to the floor of the cage, sobbing and terrified, barely able to catch my breath before it happened all over again.

I gave up counting how many times he drowned me.

When I came up the last time, he was saying something. Black spots danced across my vision as I fought for consciousness, but I could hear him speaking. I no longer found his voice charming or lovely. It was the voice of evil.

"Vines. Vines with grapes spilling out of them. Do you see it? See what she can do to even fermented grapes here? That's why you stole her for us. And that's the power we're going to bring to bear when war comes to the Faewald again. But this will be no small war. This war will end all wars that came before."

There was a cheer all around me.

My lungs, straining and weak, gasped for breath again.

My eyes fluttered open just in time to see grapevines spilling from the wine barrel, great red globes hanging in clusters from the vines.

I sank into a sticky pool of wine and unconsciousness.

"Did you kill her? If she's dead, she won't do you much good." I was surprised to wake up to Werex's voice and even more surprised to still be alive.

I was dripping wet. Someone had poured enough water through the cage to wash me and everything else so that the stickiness of the wine was gone. How thoughtful. They could have chosen to just not drown me in wine in the first place, but no, the thoughtfulness lay in washing me off afterward. Just when I thought the Faewald couldn't get worse, it taught me a new lesson in cruelty.

"They're heartier than you would think. You wouldn't imagine what paces I put her sister through after I married her. Pain refines them. Makes them better suited to this world."

Werex grunted. The cage was moving but I didn't have the energy to straighten up. I clung to the floor of the cage, freezing cold, but weak as a newborn kitten.

"You'll love this story, Werex. Let me tell it to you as we walk."

"I'd rather show you the army we have camped here," Werex replied. "If we are to be allies, we must assess our shared strengths. My Lieutenant is here with a full report."

"We're ready to march at a single shout from you, Lord Werex." A voice called in greeting. This voice sounded like a Fae woman who'd been chewing rocks for breakfast. "We're a thousand strong. Weapons ready and polished. Golems armed. Tents can be taken down and moved with a single order."

"Have you ever been tricked into marriage?" Cavariel asked the Lieutenant, a charming tone filling his voice. Did he flirt with anyone vaguely female? I couldn't hate him more than I did ... but I might try to anyway. "I would be willing to wager you've considered letting some ugly Twilight Fae trick you."

"You misjudge me, Lord of Cups," the Lieutenant growled. I didn't have to see her to hear her lip curling as she spoke. Good for her. She was in charge of an army. Why would she want some fool like Cavariel tricking her into marriage?

My cheeks felt hot. I was lying to myself. After all, hadn't I blushed and trembled at my first sight of Cavariel just like my sister had? But I knew better now. I'd never fall for appearances again.

"You don't like our fine tradition?" Cavariel asked her bluntly.

Tension rode thickly in the air. What would she say? Even I could tell that their alliance with the Court of Cups was a careful thing. If she answered wrong, they might not get their war. Maybe there was something I could say to provoke a division between them.

I sat up, coughing. Think, Allie, think!

"It's alive," Werex growled, peering at me. He seemed pleased.

"You carry it, Lieutenant," Cavariel said, idly gesturing to me. His voice dripped with arrogance. If I could have seen his face, I would have spat in it. "Take it up to the Hall. I'll take a look at your army with High Lord Werex. Put a cloth or something over the cage when you get there."

I barely caught a glimpse of the Lieutenant's face. Her cuff was thick leather trimmed in a lace that looked like dried blood. She carried the cage low, so that it bounced along her leather-clad leg as she strode forward.

"A thousand doesn't seem like much of an army," I said. Best to get her annoyed. Then I could think of a way to turn the annoyance on the Court of Cups.

She spat to the side, missing my cage by inches. "You know nothing, ensorcelled mortal. A thousand is a grand army in the Faewald. There are not many of us here. I doubt our entire population tops ten thousand. There are golems, of course, but they will not fight."

"Why not?" I asked.

"Only Fae without honor would set mindless tools against their enemies. We kill with our own hands. What thrill is there in winning without watching the pain in your enemies' eyes?"

"Oh, yes, I can see that would be a problem." I let my tone be as dry as an ancient tomb.

She was silent for a moment, so I tried again. "Why does Cavariel think you can be tricked into marrying someone. Are you known for being a fool?"

The cage shook. Oops. I may have pushed her too far.

"Be glad that my honor protects you or even that cage could not keep me from crushing you to paste."

"Well, he *did* say he thought you could be tricked."

"You know nothing, mortal. All Fae marriages start with one Fae tricking the other into the marriage. How else could you convince someone to give up their freedom? Of course, some Fae allow the trickery. But I am careful. I allow no one to catch my hand when I fall in case I accidentally give them my hand in marriage. I am careful to never speak in a way that could be interpreted as part of a marriage vow."

"It doesn't sound like a comfortable way to live," I suggested.

She snorted. "In truth, I'd rather they left me alone. I prefer the life of the Feast – good food, a large fire, a bedroll, and a good bloody fight. But tell me, if there are not tricks in your world, then how do mortals conduct such affairs?"

"We ask each other."

She pulled the cage up to look at me. Surprisingly, she looked young and lithe, though more muscular than any woman I'd seen before. Her skin was that faint green and her lower canines stuck out of her mouth, but she was still incredibly beautiful. I looked like the ugly thug, not her. She'd shaved all but a plume of black hair from her head and tattooed the skin showing with whorls and teeth. The plume of hair she'd braided in tiny braids and then braided all of those into one massive rope-like braid. She'd stained that with something that looked too much like dried blood for my taste.

"You're telling the truth," she said after a moment. "How dull. I'd rather be tricked than begged. You can't respect a person who asks for a thing. A Fae should be cunning – able to take what they want without resorting to the generosity of others – thin as that is."

"He said he tricked my sister."

Which put a new spin on things. What would it have been like to be Hulanna and come to this new world only to find yourself tricked into marriage by a Fae man set on 'putting her through paces.' I shivered.

She'd only been seventeen, too. She'd wanted more in life than a little town and a village boy. Was that really worth this kind of punishment? But then again, she'd nailed our father to a tree.

From this high, carried like a lantern, I could see the army. Their tents were laid out in tidy rows, cookfires lit but kept low. Golems bustled around the tents cooking and mending, cleaning and bearing loads. And the Fae warriors were dressed for battle, sparring in cheering clusters or gaming at low tables.

"Your warriors are impressive," I said. It wasn't a lie. The worst of them could break me in half. "I suppose you don't need many of them when each one is so powerful."

"Precisely," she said sharply.

"It's a pity that Cups values them so poorly."

"What makes you think they value us poorly?"

"Well, he's making you carry me, isn't he? And you're a commander. Shouldn't that be the job of a golem?"

I barely hid a smile at her snort of agreement.

"If I were you, I'd consider changing sides."

"I won't side with you, mortal, not even if it means bearing the insults of Cups."

"I don't mean me," I said. "What about Wings or whoever you are going to attack?"

She waved a hand dismissively. "If we attack them, it will only be a beginning skirmish. When their severed heads line our roads, we'll go where we really plan to attack."

They weren't attacking the Court of Wings?

"And where is that?" I asked. "A Court farther away?"

"You could say that," she said with a wide toothy grin. "The Court of Mortals."

Chapter Nineteen

The Court of Mortals. She meant my people. That's who they were planning to attack. My heart was racing faster than a run-away horse. I'd thought all I had to do was escape and get my father out of this torturous place. I'd been wrong. I was going to have to prevent an invasion.

How could I even do that?

I couldn't even get out of the cage.

I gritted my teeth, lost in thought as the Lieutenant carried me through the army encampment and up a rocky road to a soaring castle built in a clump of cedars. The cedars were like the pillars of the sky – a clump of about five or six of them growing closely together. Each was thicker than the largest building in my town and they soared up into the heavens. Between the boles, balconies and windows filled the gaps and a wide portcullis was lifted over the road.

Flowering vines bedecked with morning glories hung over every available surface of the walls and balconies, their blossoms larger than the warrior carrying me. They looked like delicate cups dipped in reddish wine.

"Welcome to Cups," the Lieutenant growled as we passed through the gates.

But I had no time to admire the fantastical palace. No time to savor the cedar-filled air. No time to gape at the daintily dressed Fae – both male and female as they sauntered easily on the cobbled streets, drifting between golem-run tailor shops with fanciful dresses spilling across the front window to haberdasheries with huge hats over the door or tiny inns swirling with the scents of peppermint and vanilla.

No, I needed a plan to get out of this mess and I needed one fast. I pulled my book from my pack, it was damp, but not soaked through – thank goodness! My blankets and clothing had protected the delicate pages. I strung up my clothesline, draping my clothes and blanket over it. I had to pull down the mouse hide to manage it. That, I laid across the floor of the cage like a rug and arranged the book gently in the fur.

"You're industrious," the Lieutenant observed. "Rare in a Fae. Only the Court of Twilight has the ambition to work for ourselves."

"Is that true?" I asked, pausing. "If it is, then you must have a massive advantage over the other Courts."

She huffed. "Well, it feels true most of the time. But we have little magic. We must work to obtain it from others. Even golems can't run forever without being revived."

Interesting.

A child ran across the street ahead of us and a stately Fae woman snatched his hand, pulling him back to her path. He glanced back at me and for a moment I thought he looked familiar. Like the Horsecomber family back home. How odd.

I flipped through the pages of the journal, looking for anything that could help. There was the mention of the key, of course.

"For opening and closing all locked things."

Like the cage, or the portal. I needed to get that back from Scouvrel.

This was interesting.

"I chased my daughter into the portal after she was entrapped. Her cousin, Flet, had seen it transpire from afar. With me, I brought my husband and Amelia. Both perished. I was forced to flee – barely clinging to life – without my sweet Posey. God and heavens preserve me. I did not have the strength to carry on.

"The madness took Amelia and Davin both. I think it was only my second sight that saved me, for with that, I could see clearly. My husband saw only twisted demons clawing at him from on every side and the sound of a howling wind until he could take it no more and he drove a knife into his own throat. Amelia saw wonders beyond my imagining. The glamor of the Fae, I think.

"I could see both those things for a moment if I tried to look through my usual sight, my eyes flicking back from one to the other as the glamor tried to cloak and the eyes to see. Each of them battled for me and I would have fallen with Amelia or with Davin had it not been for the gift. But each time, my second sight repelled them, showing me an image not as glorious as the glamor, but not as soul-scathing as the truth. It was enough to keep me sane – but not enough to save them.

"The Fae convinced Amelia to eat her own finger thinking it was a sweet treat before they finally killed her. I don't know if her fate was worse, or Davin's. She, at least, seemed content with the grim bargain. His spirit broke like a shattered bottle.

"I barely escaped to warn my sisters in the mortal world. We must keep this book safe. We must let each generation know of it. Without these warnings, the portal will open utterly, and our world will fall."

I shivered. A horrible story. And not entirely unlike mine.

But if only one Fae could come out of the portal for every one of us that came in, how would they lead an army through the portal? There was some safety in that, surely. Unless they'd found a way around that rule.

I hadn't realized that the Lieutenant had led me into an inner sanctum until I looked up to see we were in a Great Hall filled with windows looking out between the cedars. Cedar branches wove across the ceiling and fantastical statues of mythical creatures rose between the windows. Someone had strung emeralds on delicate chains across the ceiling. They caught the light like green prisms, refracting it around them.

A high-backed oak chair sat on a dais with a window on either side of it. Beside the oak chair was a small table. The Lieutenant set my cage there.

She looked in at me. "May we meet again when the Feast of Ravens comes."

"You should think about finding a different feast," I said. "One that won't require making me a mortal enemy."

She laughed. "All creatures are my enemies. The only question is which I will kill today."

"Have you brought the prize?" a tinkling voice rang out. Hulanna!

I hurried across the cage to where I could peek at the entrance to the Hall. Hulanna had a lot of explaining to do. Right now, I almost sympathized with the orc woman. I, too, was surrounded by enemies.

"Open the cage," my sister said. I still couldn't see her.

I made a frustrated sound in the back of my throat, but the Lieutenant sounded even more frustrated as she fought against the latch.

"It doesn't open," she said with a grunt.

"Then use your knife," Hulanna said. She sounded closer.

I dodged backward as the orc woman plunged her knife into the cage, first trying to break the lock and then trying to break the bars.

"Maybe this will help."

I snatched up the book and stuffed it in my shirt, moving as far back from the orc lieutenant as I could. My sister had given her a hammer. She swung it at the cage and the entire thing rang as the blow struck. The sound pierced through my skull like a thousand knives.

"I hope you had a better plan than force," the orc woman growled as I held my head in weakened hands. "Because if I can't budge it with blunt or blade, then no one will."

She swaggered out of the way and I finally caught a glimpse of Hulanna dressed in a shimmering emerald corset dress, her hair braided up and the tips of her ears covered in pointed gold jewelry to show off her pointed ears.

"You have a lot to explain," I told her boldly.

She shot me a poisonous glance and threw a black cloth over my cage.

"Hello?" I called.

But no one answered.

Chapter Twenty

Oh, she thought that was clever, did she?

I reached out of the cage and yanked the cloth. It fell from the cage easily.

But my sister was gone.

Frustrated, I pulled off my boots and outer jacket to dry them off. If I was going to be alone in this hall for a while, I should get them dry. The feather shirt had dried quickly and was already warm and downy again. Maybe Scouvrel knew what he was doing with it.

Would he be coming for me? Did I matter to him enough for that?

Probably not. But then again, I was worth quite the price if he could snatch me back.

I didn't like the sick feeling in my belly. It cropped up every time I thought of the Knave. Cut it out, Allie. If he's dead, that's one less enemy, right? He wasn't going to help you save your father and he wasn't going to help you save your people. He was your captor, too. He could have released you at any time. And he didn't. And that meant he was the enemy.

So why was it so hard to believe that was true?

I dug back into the book. Here was another entry. This one in a short spiky hand – the only entry in that handwriting. A careful ancestor and one who didn't say much.

"We hid a certain artifact of power. We hid it in the place where morning light first hits. A way to keep an enemy. But it carries with it a price."

Wait. She was talking about the cage! My mother had said using it carried a price! And I'd found it in the cave on the mountain where the morning light hit first.

"None can open it save the captor. Not by any means except with the Key. But we hid the Key separately."

Well, that explained why the hammer didn't work. My belly flopped like a freshly caught trout. What did that mean if Scouvrel was dead? Was I stuck in here forever? Stuck using a thimble for a bathroom and a mouse hide for a carpet? A stab of fear shot through me but I forced it away.

My eyes drifted up to look out the window where the sun was rising in the distance. The Fae would go to bed soon. The memory of that child's face filled my mind – the one I'd seen in the street. I hadn't seen any other children since I came here. A tiny population where an army of a thousand was considered sprawling. Where a couple of hundred people – the number of our village – were a court. Where golems did all the work. Where there were no children.

I felt like that should mean something to me.

I shook my head and read again in the light of the many chandeliers. Golems entered the room quietly, replacing the candles in the deer antler chandeliers with fresh ones, watering the hanging roots of plants and polishing the wooden floors, and scraping the old wax of the spent candles away. They worked in perfect silence, not seeing or caring about any other golem, fixed only on their own task.

One came up to my cage and tried to bend the bars. When that didn't work, it slipped a thimble of water through the bars.

"Thank you," I said, but it didn't answer, simply turning and leaving.

A world with no children where shambling rock figures did all the chores. Hmmm.

"The price is related to the use of it and that use should not come lightly – for any who use the cage to bind will bear a weakness on their soul that makes it easier to bind them in the same way. For in looking at evil, we are more easily tainted by it. In using power, we are more susceptible to its use."

Pithy. This must have been a real popular ancestor. So why did this make me feel like my captivity was my own fault?

I shivered. Maybe because it was. I'd just gone ahead and used the cage without asking about the price because I needed it. Just like I'd used the key because I'd needed it. Just like I'd leapt through the portal because I needed to. And I hadn't weighed the cost.

Had Hulanna weighed the cost? Was she as trapped as I was? And why wasn't she talking to me?

I let myself sigh in frustration. My plan to wait and watch wasn't doing as much as I'd hoped. It's hard to watch when you do it from a cage, hard to learn your enemies when they set you on a shelf in an empty room. Maybe I'd watched and waited enough. Maybe it was time to act. If only I could think of how to act in a way that could get me everything I needed – freedom for me and Dad. And some way to decide what to do with Hulanna.

She was evil, right? After what she did with Dad, she was evil. So what did I do about that? Did I drag her back home in front of the village council? That seemed laughable and ridiculous. What would a bunch of old men and women be able to do to the High Lady of Cups? She had access to magic now. Maybe she could even destroy our whole town. She was raising an army. A thousand might be a small number compared to the stories we heard of Queen Anabetha's forces, but it was more than enough to obliterate Skundton and everything we'd ever loved there.

Did that mean it was my job to somehow defeat her here? But there didn't seem to be any justice here for violence and murder. There was no town mayor to render judgment. No knights to come and bring order. Did that mean it was up to me to somehow end her cruelty? But how could I end it short of killing her?

I was not going to kill my sister. Not even my cruel, fae sister who wanted to use her family for power.

I heard a faint voice and froze.

"You will need to get her out of that cage to use her. I was quite clear. *One born on a single day in two halves. One half for the land. One for the air. One for the rending. One for repair.*"

"Yes, I know," my sister said. She was back! I felt a stab of guilt. After all, I'd just been wondering if I should murder her. "We're the two halves of one whole born on the same day. She's the one for the land – obviously – and I'm the one for here, the air and the things that are illusion. It's why Cavariel wanted me so badly. It's why you all need me. But the rest isn't clear. Why can't we just use her in that cage?"

"What good is anything when it's caged?"

Hulanna made a frustrated sound. "But we don't know that! We don't even know which of us rends and which repairs!"

"Which of you is going to rip your mortal world in half? I think that should be obvious, Lady of Cups. She is not the one planning to invade her Court with two of ours."

"You're not the one to interpret, remember?" Hulanna said nastily. "You're the one to speak riddles and demand they be followed."

"You should not have urged me to come here today, Lady. You've already heard my sooth. You know I may not choose your side any more than the Knave could choose the Court of Wings. We are the impartial hands of the Faewald, not the pawns in your game of power. You know this is true. Balance may only work to give to those who lack and take from those with glut. The Kinslayer exists for desperate times when only her hand can dispense justice. The Knave must stir us up to keep away stagnation. And I – the Sooth – I offer insight into the future. We are not your playthings, Lady. We are the playthings of the Faewald itself."

The Kinslayer dispensed judgment? Then perhaps that was who I could bring my sister to. Perhaps that would be my next move.

There was a shuffling sound and then boots ringing across the wooden floor. I jammed the book into my shirt, pulled my boots on and stood up as fast as I could.

"Don't scramble on my account," Hulanna said, sitting gracefully on the edge of the oak throne and leaning on the arm so that her face filled my view.

I'd forgotten how beautiful she was. If anything, the Faewald had granted her greater beauty.

My heart hammered. This was the time – time to try to turn her back to us. And if it didn't work ... then the Kinslayer.

"Set Father free and I'll tell you how to get me out of this cage," I said boldly. I might only get one chance to strike a bargain.

Hulanna's smile was not kind.

"I may bargain with you yet, sister, but our father's freedom won't be the price. I require his constant blood and for that, I must have his living body."

I could feel the horror filling my expression and I couldn't stop it. To do that to her own father? "What have they done to you?"

"Don't judge me," she hissed. "Don't you ever judge me you weak, pathetic mortal."

"You were mortal once, too," I said. "Do you remember? We were best friends. A week before we went through this portal we braided each other's hair and you told me about how you were thinking about going down to the cities by the sea to work at the castle of Queen Anabetha."

She laughed harshly. "I dreamed of being a servant and you thought you were my friend because you encouraged that? Pathetic! Look at me now, Allie Hunter. I am no one's servant."

"Instead you're a villain. Stealing from the life of your own family to feed your power."

Her face looked powerful. She looked years older than me – like a woman in her twenties and not the teenage girl who had left me only a seven-day ago.

"For the first five years that I was in the Faewald, I still thought like you," she said with a twist to her mouth. "But time changes a person. And with a little change of perspective, the world can spin and suddenly you see everything differently. Do you think I like taking the tiny spark of mortal life from you and your father? Do you think I revel in your pain? But what are you to me? You are a lesser species now. A tiny, guttering flicker of a dying firefly beside the blaze of my life. If I take from you, if I use you – well, you would have been used up anyway and for less of a good reason. All mortals are. You sacrifice your own selves for weak ambitions, unrequited loves, and sad obsessions. You're too weak to even twist. Instead, you shatter."

"Leave this twisted place and come home," I begged. "Mother is missing you. We could be a family again."

Her laugh was not one born of humor. "Do you think that your 'home' is any different, Allie? Didn't you see how the people of the town each had their place and their power? Our traditions locked us in place. We were born into a backwater town we would never leave. Born into roles we had no choice over. You know this, Allie. You're only a Hunter because your father was and because you aren't pretty enough to marry a good catch. Olen was your only chance at anything else and Heldra had her claws in him. He'd never get away from her. You know this. How can you be so stupid that you never saw it?"

"How can you be so stupid that you think evil is the best way to change that?" I shot back. "You want to march an army into our world and tear it apart! You want to kill our friends. You kidnapped me! You nailed our father to a tree. And for what?" I was yelling now. "For beauty and power and pretty dresses and a pretty man and jewels and palaces and ..."

"And *what*, Allie?" There was venom in her tone, but I kept on going.

"He doesn't even love you! He bragged about trapping you!"

She slapped her hand down on the table beside the cage so hard that it shook me like an earthquake. She was shaking, her perfect Fae face blushing.

"You're jealous, Allie. You've always been jealous of me. You're jealous that people like me. Jealous that people think I'm prettier than you and better than you. And now you're jealous that it's all true – because I'm immortal and immortally beautiful and I always will be."

Of course, I was. Who wouldn't be?

She wasn't done. "And you should have been even more jealous. You know how you spent the past few years hoping for a dance with Olen Chanter, maybe even a kiss? I had those kisses behind his father's woodshed. You know how you were thinking about becoming the Hunter someday? Alen Tentrees was talking to our father just days before I came here. He wanted his son to be Hunter and marry me. Dad was thinking about it. You weren't going to have anything, Allie. Not anything. You should have been so much more jealous. You should have been furious. You still should be."

And I was. Worse than that, I was furious with her. Because she knew everything I'd ever wanted, and she was smashing it to bits before my eyes.

"Why didn't you tell me?" I asked, fighting against a tremble in my jaw. "If you were my friend – why didn't you say something? Why did you kiss the boy I loved? We were raised in the same home with parents who loved us. How you turn into such an awful shrew?"

Her expression turned mocking. "How could I turn out to be awful while you're so good? Are you really that good, Allie? Stop and think. Your father came into this world calling for you. Why couldn't he find you? Why did you leave him to a terrible torturous death in the Faewald? You helped me dance and call the Fae when you were supposed to be doing your chores. And I bet the town asked you not to come here. I bet they ordered you not to – that would be just like them – and I bet you did it anyway. Are you really so much better than I am, Allie?

"We all have a seed of darkness growing in us. It's just that yours is wizened and pathetic, a tiny plant, like all the tiny plants in your garden. But mine is tall and powerful and magnificent. I'm better than you at everything – even at being awful.

"And I'm the only one who ever wanted more for you, you ungrateful little idiot. Why do you think I bartered with those traveling people for a better future for us? Why do you think I came here? You can live here with me. You can stop being a jealous, ugly echo of me and actually have your own power. With glamor, you could even be beautiful. You could trick someone into marrying you. You could be the one to be enchanted by pretty dresses and glorious jewels."

I'd only ever wanted to be the Hunter. But I could hunt here, couldn't I? There were interesting creatures here – things I'd never seen before. I could protect the courts from them. If everything she said was true, then I'd been betrayed by my family first. By my father who had been willing to sell my birthright. By my mother who had let me use the cage without warning me what could happen. By Olen – but I already knew that. Sort of.

Hulanna's eyes glittered. "Just open up that cage and step out here with me."

There it was.

And that was why I couldn't trust her at all. Because she didn't really want to give me a better life. She hadn't even been willing to speak to me before. Not until it became clear that she wouldn't be able to rip me out of the cage and use me against my will.

This was all about power for her.

And the most powerful thing you could ever do was refuse to be used.

"No," I said.

Her smile turned cruel.

"I'll let you think about it. You can think about it alongside your father. Maybe watching him suffer right in front of your eyes will lure you out. Or maybe you're too jealous and heartless to do this even for him."

She pulled something out of a pocket in her dress and held it up for me to see – a glowing seed.

She tossed it on the ground beside my cage and a golden oak erupted out of it, growing as if centuries had elapsed over a single second. With a sound like a *pop* my father emerged from the tree, still nailed to it through his shoulders. He panted for breath, blood bubbling from his nose and mouth.

"Please, Hulanna," I begged. "Let him go. Take those nails out!"

"Come out of the cage and do it yourself, Allie." She rose from the throne.

"I can't do that. Please! If you have any pity!"

His head lolled to the side. Was he unconscious? The smell of his blood filled my nose.

"It's up to you now, Allie. If you want him free, come out of the cage." She smiled cruelly. "I'll leave you to think about it."

And then she was striding out of the room, her emerald satin dress flowing around her like a mocking flag, and my sight was blurred by the tears flooding my eyes.

How could she do this to our father?

Chapter Twenty-One

"Dad!" I gasped. I shoved my head through the bars, but try as I might, I couldn't reach him.

His eyes were closed, his lashes tangled in a crust of blood. His head hung down, his hair hanging in a rough tangle around his face. From my low position on the table, I could just make out the pained twist of his mouth and the slight moisture dripping from his nose. His lips were thick and swollen, his eyes dark with bruising. He mumbled something unintelligible through his cracked lips.

He was probably thirsty. And I couldn't get him a drink.

Only magic could be keeping him alive. His blood leaked, thick and viscous, down from the spikes in his shoulders. His legs were buckled at his knees, his whole weight borne by the spikes in his flesh. My stomach twisted at the sight of them. Dirty and stinking, his clothing was old and dried blood coated his face and beard. No one had attended to his needs for days. The way the blood pooled in his limp fingers told me he couldn't use his arms to help himself.

I choked on a sob, trembling at the sight of him.

In all my life, I'd never met anyone stronger than my dad. He was stronger than the giant cedars outside. He was invincible.

Except that he wasn't.

I let out a shuddering sob.

"Can you hear me?" I whispered.

He whispered something unintelligible and I wiped my cheeks with a hand, pushing my tears away. Hulanna thought it was jealousy that motivated me, did she? I couldn't deny that there was a slither of that inside me. But the real fire that rose within wasn't jealousy. It was rage. A rage so powerful it burned through me like a fire, consuming everything unnecessary, driving out fear and jealousy and anxiety and leaving only the fire of fury.

She thought this would motivate me to help her? She was wrong. The only thing I wanted now was to destroy her.

She wanted my father's blood? I would give her blood. I would soak her world in it.

I would tear it to the ground. I would –

The sound of small voices filled the air and I watched as a door on the other end of the room opened and a quiet golem led a line of crying children behind him. There were five of them. The first two, I recognized. They were from Skundton. The Earthmover baby – the two-year-old my father had found in the woods. The Delving boy – Nils. He was five. Though he looked older. My heart skipped a beat. Had I been here long enough that the child had aged? I didn't know the next two. Two girls as dirty as the others, maybe seven-years-old. And then a little boy of about four with huge eyes and a face that was the spitten image of Olen at that age.

I gasped, but the crying children didn't see me, and the golems opened another door and led them away.

They had human children here. I couldn't think of a more horrible place to bring a child – far from the arms of the ones who loved them, brought fearful and alone to this terrible tangled place. With every ache I felt for my father, I felt one for them, too.

I had something more to add to my list, now. Free my father. Stop Hulanna. Free the children.

This had to end. One horror was compounded by the next, but if they thought they were going to bend Alastra Hunter into submission, they could think again.

I would not go easily.

And now I knew that my sister carried my father's suffering body and that tree around in her pocket in the form of a glowing seed. If I could only escape, I could find her and steal that seed to free him. I could find a way to save those children.

I just needed to listen. I just needed to watch.

A golem came through another door and I braced for what horror he would bring. But he only carried a scrap of paper between two blocky fingers. His footfalls were surprisingly light for something so large. My father's eyes flickered open for a moment.

"Dad? Can you hear me?"

"Allie," he mumbled. His eyes flickered closed again and again his words were garbled and then gone.

"Dad, I love you. Please hold on."

I couldn't tell if he heard me.

When I turned around, the scrap of paper was in my cage, the written letters as large as my fist.

Lady of Cups has a secret meeting arranged with the Lord of Silk two days hence at the Bridge of Reasoning.

And what good would knowing that do me? Very little. But if nothing else, it told me I might have an ally here.

"I'm going to get out of here somehow, Dad," I whispered. "And when I do, I'm coming for you. One way or another, I'm coming for you and I'm going bring you home."

But what was I going to do about all the rest?

I'd been in training to be the Hunter my whole life. I'd fought for the right to protect my people from bears and cougars lurking in the forest. I'd fought off hordes of carrion ghouls waiting to catch a defenseless goat or child. I'd fought to fend off starvation when the flocks were insufficient and the autumn harvest was dwindling, to pull in deer and rabbits to fill aching bellies.

But I'd never realized that our greatest enemy was lurking the whole time just out of reach. I hadn't realized that by going with my sister to the circle and dancing, I'd betrayed them all. I'd created a beast that was worse than any other, a threat that was sure to wipe my people from life like a woman with a mop cleans a spill on the floor.

I swallowed.

But this time when my hands shook it was with determination.

I was done hunting bears and cougars. I was done with ghouls. I was going to hunt Fae. Yeah, I'd said that before. I'd meant it before, but never more than here beside my bleeding father who had suffered to come after me. Never more than seeing those innocent children with round ears – mortal children with flushed cheeks and tearful eyes.

I couldn't afford to be angry or afraid for myself anymore. There were other people who needed that more.

Carefully, I cleaned up my clothing, rearranged my pack and jamming the note in the bottom of it. Then I sat down with the book again. I was scanning again. Avoiding personal stories, looking for anything that might have some kind of relevance to getting out of here.

"We can only theorize about the magic that binds the circle in place. It did not come from our world, though we put up stones to mark the place. Stones to keep idle feet from wandering in. Stones to tell our Chanter where to wait and play. Playing music helps. We learned that early on. The music is partly to dazzle the Fae. But it's partly for us. It gives us strong, brave hearts and that seems to counter their magic. Frana had a theory about their magic and the circle. I've searched the records trying to confirm it. I think it may be true. When negative emotions swell in our town, we seem to call them. If someone enters their realm, the calling becomes more powerful – or if we dance there, willing them to come.

If someone denies them, meaning it in their heart, then that pushes them away.

"They feed off emotion. Our pain. Our anger. Our desperation fuels them. The more pain, the tastier the treat. We don't know what they do with those they take – but we suspect they must torture them. Any mortals we've found after were woefully treated. Most, lost their minds in the process. All, were rent with scars. They must feed off our agony. So why not cause as much agony as possible?

"To that end, we women keep these things hidden, passed down only to those mature enough to understand – we must keep them away. We must not let our youth be tempted by them. Better to believe they are superstitions. Better to think they are only Faeries stories."

Well, the old ladies hadn't considered what would happen if people thought Fae were Faeries stories and called them by accident, did they? Because that's what happened with me and Hulanna and now we're here.

Or was that an accident? Hulanna had been very insistent that morning. And she claimed she'd been trying to get us a better life. Had she known this was real? Had she planned it?

I shivered.

I'd only learned two things. One wouldn't do me much good – trying to calm down was not an option.

The other was that I should use music more.

I began to hum lightly under my breath, letting the old lullabies of my childhood drift through the air, dropping from my lips like pearls.

My father seemed to calm at the sound, his breath growing less labored. I hummed until I drowsed against the bars and drifted off to sleep.

I woke to Hulanna's voice.

"Wake up, Allie."

"I'm awake," I said thickly, blinking as I tried to remember where I was. It was still day. I couldn't have slept for long.

Hulanna held something up and I blinked as I climbed to my feet and stepped closer to the bars. She shoved the thing toward me and I stepped back, horrified.

It was a Fae ear, smeared in dried blood.

"What is that?" I choked. "You didn't cut off your own – "

My words cut off as I recognized the tattoo on the ear. A feather. Climbing up to the tip of it. I'd seen that once before.

"Of course not," Hulanna said, and there was something strange in her eyes. "We Fae prize our ears. They're a symbol of our strength and our beauty. Any Fae with only one ear would be a disgrace – a hideous monster. Too weak to live. No one could take my ear short of killing me."

"And did you ..." my words died in my throat and I had to cough to get my voice back. "Did you kill the owner of that ear?"

Her eyes were far too bright.

"All your allies are gone, Allie. They're meaningless. You have no one who can help you. Stop fighting me. Come out of the cage and join me. Together, we will reshape the world. I can forgive you. I can take you back as my twin sister. We can do this together. Just open the cage."

"I can't," I said in a small voice, almost grateful for that right now. If I could, then I'd be out there with her. And she'd probably nail me to a tree. But if I could get out, I could free my father.

She set the ear on the arm of the chair with a look of disgust.

"Stop thinking about what you can't do and start thinking about what will be done to you if you don't," she said. "I swear, Allie. I can hardly believe you're my twin."

I started to sing – a song about home and fire about tucking in close to the blaze while the winds howled around you – and she spun with a growl.

"Stop."

As if I would stop because she commanded me. In a fit of pique, I sang louder, crashing into the chorus about the howling of the wind and the roar of the blaze – and she froze, mesmerized. I could see the struggle behind her eyes as she fought against the music. She shook herself and spun quickly, slapping my father across the face.

I gasped, my song faltering, and her eyes lit brighter.

"Sing again, and I'll do worse."

I was still gaping at her when she left the room.

Chapter Twenty-Two

When I woke, someone had put the black cloth over the cage again. My thimble was full of water. I drank, refilling my waterskin, and then tried to pull the fabric off the cage. It didn't budge this time.

The cage moved.

"Hello?" I called.

There was no answer but the sound of feet on a dirt surface and the calls of night birds in the trees.

I began to hum again.

Something shook the cage and I fell from my feet.

I began to sing again but this time, the cage was shaken so hard that I smashed into the bars. Ouch! Pain flared in my jaw and I touched it tenderly. There was going to be a bruise.

But I'd learned my lesson. No singing. With a sigh, I pulled the blanket from my pack and wrapped it around me, nestling down into the mouse fur rug. It was getting colder. I had a bad feeling that I'd been separated from my father again. And I hadn't even had the chance to really talk to him.

Stay calm, Allie. Don't cry. They love it when you suffer. So, don't suffer.

I kept telling myself that until I drifted to sleep again.

I woke suddenly when the cloth was ripped off the cage.

"Haunt me, Little Nightmare," a voice cooed, and my breath whooshed out of my lungs. I slumped to my knees.

"Scouvrel!"

He was alive. He was alive and staring at me with hungry eyes like he wanted to eat me.

"You've been prancing all over the Faewald without me," he said smoothly, a single eyebrow lifting. "When you're inside it, doesn't it look vast and glorious? I hate to break it to you, but once you've left it's only broken teacups and muddy ribbons scattered over the moss."

"I thought you were dead." My heart hurt it was beating so hard. I would have thought relief would have felt more pleasant.

A dangerous glimmer of something like hurt filled his eyes. "And are you sorry that I am not?"

"How ... how am I here?"

Here seemed to be a library. There were shelves around us full of books, a roaring fire in a fireplace with stuffed chairs ringing it and on the table my cage was set on, there was a platter of cheese and fruit.

Scouvrel followed my gaze and his head turned, revealing a bloody bandage.

"It was really your ear!" I said, shocked, my hand rushing to cover my mouth.

"I've never been fond of these ears," Scouvrel said in a manner deceptively casual, lifting the cage so that I could see all around us. I tried to drink in the library from the perspective of something the size of a book. The bookcases went up so high that a ladder leaned against the nearest one. The books disappeared into the darkness above us. "They put one in mind of the jackrabbit – not predator, but prey. I have long wished to shed the implication."

My laugh had a hysterical edge to it. "And so you dismembered yourself? Is that it?"

He gave me a long, searching look and I found I could not watch the books, I was trapped by his glittering eyes, by the way his full lips pressed together as he studied me. By the way it seemed he might search my very soul. Eventually, when he spoke, his words were graver than I was used to.

"I paid a price to get you back – and a fair one. With the added benefit that now I need only listen to half your ramblings."

"You gave your ear up for *me*?" Should I be horrified by his sacrifice? Or perhaps grateful? I didn't know which to feel. Why would he do that? Surely, whatever price he got in auctioning me wasn't worth the price of his own ear!

"Don't flatter yourself, Nightmare. The ear is the most expendable of organs."

"Hulanna said that the Fae treasure their ears."

He coughed awkwardly, confirming she'd been right. His eyes held a haunted look despite his cool manner. I was used to teasing Scouvrel and nasty Scouvrel. I was not used to cold, prickly Scouvrel.

"And you've been busy. Is that a rat hide you've been rolling all over?" He was stalking through his library as if he were looking for something. "If I had known how much you enjoyed life with the rats, perhaps I would not have bothered to barter for your return."

"What is *that*?" I asked, pointing to the painting he'd stopped in front of. It was painted on parchment tacked to a board. But there were no paints visible. Someone had taken time to paint what looked like the swirling clouds around the moon entirely in a dark maroon paint.

I froze.

"I painted it for you, Nightmare. We'll have to leave it here. It won't fit in the cage. But I thought you might appreciate it. After all, you're a bloody little thing."

"Is that painted in blood?" I couldn't quite keep the horror from my voice.

"Well, I wasn't going to give away my ear without getting a little more use out of it first."

I felt my mouth hanging open, but I couldn't shut it. He spun to stare into the cage, his dark eyes flashing in his perfectly beautiful face. Predators were always more beautiful than their prey. I'd never wondered why before.

It was easy to forget that Scouvrel wasn't human. Easy until moments like this. My hand wavered just touching my blindfold, almost wanting to tug it up and see his tangled body again as a way to remind myself that he wasn't a mortal like me. He wasn't plagued with soft human emotions. I looked at my feet, almost afraid to meet his eyes.

"You painted something in your own blood for *me*?"

He didn't speak until I looked up into his devouring gaze.

"Yes, *you*, Nightmare. You have haunted me night and day and now I will haunt you."

"It seems grisly," I said gently.

"Have you forgotten that we aren't mortal, Little Nightmare?" he whispered. "When I found someone in the Court of Twilight who would deal with me, humiliation was the only currency he would take."

I swallowed.

"I am grateful that you bought me back."

"We're allies," he shrugged, but his shoulders slumped as he began to walk away from the painting. Was he seriously disappointed that I didn't like his ... art? It was painted in his own blood!

I shook my head. I did not understand the Fae.

"I don't appreciate great art," I said, trying to comfort him. "I grew up in a village far from the Queen's Court. To an experienced eye, I'm sure the painting would be stunning."

"You do appreciate sacrifice though, I would expect," he snapped.

Had I hurt his feelings? Was that possible?

I licked my lips and tried to make my tone as gentle as I could. "I am very grateful for your enormous sacrifice. Thank you."

He tilted his head like he was considering it. "I don't just *give* things away without a trade, you know."

"What would you have me trade?" I asked, trying not to laugh at his wounded dignity. "I have a very fine rat skin on offer."

His eyes sparkled with an emotion somewhere between rage and offended hurt.

"I was thinking of a kiss," he said in a hiss.

"You like to trade for those a lot," I said, fighting my fear and surprise. Why that? Why now?

He gave me a suspicious look. "Is that a no?"

"How could I say no when you have given such a prized possession on my behalf?"

I needed to get back in his good favor. I needed him to let me out. I needed to go find my sister and get that golden seed.

If a kiss did that, of course I'd give it. And I didn't dare hurt his feelings or he'd keep me in here forever and then how would I free those children or my father?

He set the cage on the table, his eyes burning with some emotion I couldn't read. Was he breathing faster?

"I've thought of you constantly since you left me, Nightmare. I wish I could be rid of the thought of you."

What did you even say to that? I'd thought of him, too. Mostly because I was worried he was dead and I'd never get out of the cage.

"Do you want out of your cage?" he asked, his eyes smoldering.

"Yes," I gasped. More than anything. "You can let me out. You can."

"Agree not to try to escape when I let you out. Agree not to harm me or kill me," he said. He really was breathing too quickly. He wasn't ... excited ... was he? Maybe he liked danger. Maybe he liked the idea that I might try to harm him.

"I agree," I said, and he opened the latch.

Chapter Twenty-Three

I sprang from the cage. I hadn't expected so many emotions to hit me at once. I gasped in a long breath, shuddering as the sensation of pure freedom shot through me. I was out of the cage. Some small part of myself hadn't believed that would ever happen again.

I'd barely drawn a breath when his arms were around me, catching me as I stumbled from the surprise of being full-sized again. It felt surprisingly good to be held by someone who cared about me – cared in his own, strange way. He swept me up against him, leaning in and taking a kiss from me. His kiss felt sad and desperate, longing and hopeful. It was gentle, not forcing anything, but waiting for my response. And his lips stayed on mine for longer than necessary, as if he were lingering, savoring the kiss.

It left me utterly confused.

Even with the slowness of it, he was done too quickly. I felt a pang of almost physical pain when he stepped away.

"I don't want to go back in the cage."

His eyes met mine and something like warmth blossomed in them.

"Then bargain with me to stay out for a while," he said with a half-smile. He took a step closer, breathing me in like a flower.

"You seemed to enjoy that kiss," I suggested awkwardly. Because why did he enjoy kissing me so much? No one else did.

Even Olen had only kissed me because his mother told him to. Did they draw magic from positive emotions, too?

"I did." His grin was widening.

My cheeks were hot. Even my neck felt like it was burning. I was not good at this. Give me something to kill and I was your girl. Give me someone to kiss and it tangled me up in knots. Oh, stars and heavens! Tangled. An image of his tangled body flashed through my mind and my stomach rolled violently inside me. I fought against the wave of nausea.

"What if I bargained one more kiss for an hour out of the cage," I said, breaking out into a sweat along my spine. "I need food. I need to feel mortal for just an hour. And I need to talk with you."

"No escaping. No violence to me. No trying to leave this room," he cautioned, but the eager look in his eyes told me he wanted this bargain, too.

"Agreed," I said, and his smile sent a little thrill through me.

"Let's eat," he waved a hand to the food on the tray like a generous host.

I sat carefully on the edge of one of the chairs – I was definitely the worse for wear – and grabbed the closest chunk of cheese, pausing just before it reached my mouth.

"I need salt," I said.

He laughed – a genuine belly laugh. "That's another myth. You don't need salt to eat our food. It won't bind you here. We will bind you here, not our food."

I ignored the threat hanging in the air, shutting my eyes in bliss as I ate the cheese. I was ravenous. When I opened my eyes, he was watching me like a cat, his eyes huge and irises blown wide.

"Tasty?" he asked lightly.

"I'm so hungry," I said, grabbing a handful of nuts and dried fruit from the tray and putting them all in my mouth.

"No need to rush, Little Hunter. I did make you a promise that I would never let you go hungry. I prepared this tray for you to keep that bargain."

"I need," I tried to say but had to wait a moment until all the food was swallowed. "I need to talk to you about letting me out of the cage."

"Why don't you finish eating," he said, gesturing to a silk screen on the other side of the room. "And cleaning yourself. I arranged for fresh clothing and a small bath behind that screen. You might even like it. Those other clothes look ... worn."

Worn was a generous word for how ruined my clothing was.

"I'm not here for clothes and baths," I said. "They have children in their Court. Mortal children."

He just watched me, considering. He didn't say anything. No surprise. No horror.

"You knew." The food fell from my hand. Why did I feel betrayed? He was Fae. He was cruel. He was twisted. I knew that. So why had I expected him to care?

"It's a common thing to steal mortal children," he said eventually. "We can't make our own anymore."

My jaw dropped open. I shut it with a snap. I'd kissed him. I'd kissed someone this heartless.

"You don't care. They're stealing children and you don't care."

He looked both puzzled and nervous like he feared my reaction and didn't know what it was going to be.

I felt the heat on my cheeks before I realized I was crying. Why had I seen him as a friend? Because he gave me food and gross gory paintings? Because he liked to bargain with me for kisses?

I must never forget that he wasn't human, that he wasn't my friend.

"You're a monster." I stood up. I had to get away from him. My vow kept me in the room, but I didn't need to sit across from him like a friend.

I backed up until my shoulders hit a solid bookcase behind me. My jaw was trembling. My tears were flowing hot and fast so that my vision blurred.

Scouvrel's hands were held up, like he was trying to pacify me. "I told you we were monsters."

"You're not going to let me go to save them?" They were just children. Just scared children with no one to take care of them.

"No." His words were quiet. Like stabbing me in the back was no great thing to bother about.

"You're not going to free me to save my father either, are you?" My voice was getting thick from tears. I didn't care.

"Absolutely not."

"Then why buy me back at all? Why not just leave me with my sister?"

He swallowed and his eyes looked haunted as he said, "I'm the Knave of Courts. I sow trouble. It's what I do."

"I hate you." My hands were shaking. My knife was in my hand despite my vow. I crossed the room to where he stood in two steps and had it to his throat in another breath. I ignored his bloody ear. His sacrifice wasn't for me. It was for some game he was playing.

He didn't care about scared children. He didn't care about my suffering father. He didn't care because they were mortals, just like me. He didn't think we were owed compassion or respect.

I would show him otherwise.

"What do you want from me, Alastru Livoto Hunter?" He sounded tired.

"I want you to *respect* me!" I was shouting. I couldn't stop. It was like I was a dog let free from my leash.

"I respect the knife you hold to my throat." His eyes were bright.

"Not good enough." Another hot tear, running down my face.

"I respect the violence in your eyes."

"I want so much more than that." I was shaking so hard that the knife point trembled.

"I respect the life in your beating heart that demands my suffering."

"That may suffice."

I pulled the knife away before I could break my vow. If I could break my vow.

"I just have to save my father and those children. That's all."

He cleared his throat, his fingers skimming where my knife had been. "I respect *that*."

"But you won't help me?" I asked. I was full-blown crying now and I couldn't even stop it.

"No."

"Kisses are wasted on you. So are threats," I said, sheathing the knife. "You have no heart to break. You have no soul to harm."

I could have spat on him right then and there. But why waste the energy?

I pulled up my blindfold to remind me of who he really was.

"Please, don't – " He raised a hand, pleading, but all I saw was a tangled travesty of raw nerves and inner distress.

I stalked behind the screen, stripped off my dirty clothing, and dropped into the hot water, scrubbing myself with all the fury I couldn't unleash anywhere else and letting my tears flow unchecked.

When I came out of the wooden tub, my skin was red and the room was silent except for the occasional splash of water against the side of the tub.

Scouvrel was no friend of mine.

Which meant I could not afford to feel anything for him but hatred. I would have to best him just like I would have to best my sister. I might have to kill him. Maybe I should do that now, while I had the chance.

The memory of his dismembered ear danced before my eyes, but I shoved it away. Who knew why he did that? It certainly hadn't been to help me.

I dressed angrily in the clothes he'd laid out. Sleek boots entirely made of black crow feathers climbing up to my knees, a matching delicate jacket made of owl feathers with a high, frothy owl-feather collar. A pair of soft tan leather fitted trousers and a frothy white top edged in lace. At least there were no dresses. I'd feel like a fool in a gown.

But it felt wrong to let him dress me when I wanted nothing so much as to tear his eyes from his head. I glanced at the dirty clothes on the floor. I couldn't put them back on. They were stained with wine and rat blood. Ruined completely. With a sigh, I marched out of the area behind the screen, trying not to look like I was pleased with my new clothing.

Scouvrel was standing right in front of me, arms crossed over his broad chest and a single perfect eyebrow raised.

"In a temper?" he asked frostily.

"I'll never forgive you for your black heart," I said, mirroring his coldness.

"I was stolen as a child and brought here. Just like those children." Embers of something close to fury flickered in his eyes.

I felt like someone hit me in the belly.

"Don't think you know what a thing like that is like," he went on. "Trust me. Your captivity has been a lovely seaside visit in comparison."

"Then you're twice as wicked not to help me now," I said, letting the acid flow in my words. "You know what it's like for them and you just don't care. You're heartless. You're twisted. You're nothing."

His lip twisted angrily and he crossed the room to me in a single stride. Grabbing my collar, he pulled me roughly to him so suddenly that I plunged the dagger toward him. He caught my wrist with his hand, twisting it until I dropped the knife, holding my gaze with his furious one. A moment passed with us locked in place like that, both breathing hard and then he leaned in to kiss me – gently, like a butterfly landing. I couldn't help it when my traitor heart galloped at the touch. His kiss felt like robbery and a gift all at the same time. It was over before it began. Aching pain passed over his face when he was done and a cruel glint flashed in his eye. He scooped up my knife, shoved the hilt into my hand, and with one motion he shoved me back toward the cage and shut the door on me.

Scooping up a handful of nuts and fruit, he tossed them through the bars after me. I barely got my arms up in time to deflect an almond before it hit me. It was as large as a chunk of hewn wood for the fire and just as heavy. I bit back a curse at the pain that flared in my arm. That was certainly going to bruise.

I had bruises everywhere and nothing to show for them. I even had bruises in my ensorcelled heart.

He strode out of the room without looking back, slamming the door to the library behind him and leaving me shaking like a leaf in my new feather boots.

How did you handle a man like that? Was there even a way?

Oddly, I thought that perhaps Hulanna might have known what to do. But since that would end in destroying our world, I didn't want to find out.

I sat in my cage, alone and heartbroken realizing that nothing was what I thought it was. Not my town. Not my family. Not my ally here in the Faewald. Maybe not even me.

Chapter Twenty-Four

I'd been practicing my speech and the moment he returned, I threw it at him.

"You told me that your kind doesn't lie, but what you meant was that you're better at it than we are. You lie in every false note of your voice, every sidelong glance, every time your breath hitches in promise. You lie with each true word you say."

He stopped, one hand on his hip as if to show off how his shirt was unbuttoned all the way to his belt. Why would I care that he was physically perfect when that was all glamor? I'd seen the real him, tangled and ridiculous.

"What have I ever said to make you think otherwise?" He paused. "Hatred for me?"

I'd forgotten we were playing that game. "Five."

His expression morphed into a feral smile. "Perfect. Readiness for adventure?"

I hesitated. What kind of adventure? The way he was smirking at me had me worried. "Four."

"I'd offer you a cloak as it's chilly by the sea, but I don't have one small enough. You'll have to wear that detestable rat rug if you need it."

"Or you could let me out of the cage."

"Think again. I bribed someone sympathetic at the Twilight Court to give you back to me, but the Balance of Courts is still taking bids on you and it suits my purposes to continue that game. You know that the Law of Games makes it impossible to break off a game once it has begun. I will not defy that law any more than I'll defy my own nature."

"That didn't stop the Court of Twilight or the Court of Cups," I said acidly.

"No, that was the Court of Cup's bid. Balance wrote it down after the fact. A bid of one game-interrupting theft. Not a very high bid, but it was the highest at the time."

"That's higher than an entire castle?" I said, shock in my voice as he scooped up the cage and I scrambled to secure my dried fruit and almonds.

"Depends on the castle."

"Willingness to tell me what you're actually doing, Scouvrel?"

"One," he said with a teasing smirk. His fury of before had faded, replaced with his usual mockery and teasing. But I'd never forget the way he'd kissed me and thrown me in the cage or the hurt and fury in his eyes as he spoke of his own origins.

"We aren't just going on an adventure. You didn't just do all this work to mess with the other Courts – even if that is kind of your job."

"Role. Not job. I don't work. Ruining things for everyone else is my *role*."

"Like in a play?"

"Life is one huge act."

He strode out the door, my cage swinging in his hand. It opened to ... nothing. All I could see was gray, cloudy sky.

Before I could gasp, his wings unfurled in smoky clouds around us and he leapt.

I'd seen smoke waterfalls. I'd seen the Tanglewood and tiny nests in the willows. I'd seen cedar castles and pavilion encampments. I hadn't seen this yet.

I jammed my head out of the cage, ignoring the way my heart did flip flops as we plunged down towards a tattered cloud. My attention was fully fixed on the place we'd just left.

It was a soaring statue – taller than any mountain I'd ever seen. A statue of a massive, robed skeleton clutching a sword in both hands. The sword tip plunged toward the ground. The shoulders of the statue were heavy as if the hooded cloak it wore was disguising stubs of wings. We'd emerged out of the eye of the statue. A crown hung from a rakish angle on its head.

I gasped as we hit the clouds and the statue vanished in the mist. It had been horrifying ... and utterly impressive. How had Scouvrel brought all those books up there? Or the water for my bath?

"Enjoyment of your role?" I whispered.

"Until this seven-day, I would have said five." His voice was uncharacteristically sober.

"And now?"

"One."

His 'one' was almost lost in the thick white blanket.

"You're going to hit the ground. I can't see a thing."

"Everything is always shrouded. The key is to know where it is without looking."

"Listen," I said, trying to be as reasonable as anyone could be in a world that was full of twisted creatures, statues of colossal skeletons and constant games and trickery. "You say that you want me to be your ally. You say that you want me to help you defeat my sister. But I can't figure out what you want from me. You want to keep me in a cage. You want to sell me to the highest bidder. How does any of that help you get what you want?"

He was silent, flying through the fog like he wasn't even listening.

"Fine," I said. "Why don't I offer you an idea? My sister is holding my father captive. You said you won't free me to go and rescue him. But she says that his suffering is essential to her plans and she keeps him as a golden seed in her pocket. Why don't you snatch him away from her? If you really want to screw things up for her, why not take something that she needs?"

Eventually, he spoke, though the fog muted his voice. This whole landscape felt dreamlike.

"That would be an admirable goal, if I had any idea where she was."

We broke through a bank of clouds and now the world below could be seen like small green islands in a sea of filmy white.

"Have you ever heard of a place called the Bridge of Reasoning?"

We dropped slightly in the sky and I scrambled to cling to the bars.

"Scouvrel? Are you hurt?"

"Who gave you that name?" he demanded.

I couldn't see his face as he tied the cage to his belt. Great. It was going to be so easy to convince him to let me in on his plans when I couldn't even see his face.

"Someone slipped me a paper when I was kidnapped. It said that the Lady of Cups was going to meet the Lord of Silk – whoever that is – in two days at the Bridge of Reasoning."

"How many days ago was that?"

"One maybe? I don't know. People aren't exactly kind to me in here. They drown me in wine barrels and put a cloth over my cage."

"They," he stopped, and his voice sounded almost strangled when he continued. "They drowned you in a wine barrel?"

"How else did you think my clothing got stained with wine? Apparently, it's great fun to drown a person over and over again."

"We could go to the Bridge of Reasoning. Your logic isn't flawed. Crippling your sister's goals in any way will certainly suit my own desires."

We twisted in the wind.

"We're going there now? Where were we going to go before I said something?"

"To make trouble." His laugh was genuine. Almost as light as it had been when he was the one in the cage. Strange that he seemed freer then and more burdened now. "But this is better trouble."

We flew in silence for long minutes before I said, "You should trust me with your plan. What good am I as an ally if I don't even know why you're working with me?"

"Perhaps I crave your ignorance."

"Then get used to disappointment. I will find out. Eventually."

"Perhaps I do not trust someone who hates me."

"Then you should try to be more loveable."

He laughed.

We soared through the air. It wasn't bright enough to read, so I ate dried fruit and thought until eventually Scouvrel spoke again.

"Your sister wants to combine you with her in some way and use you both to attack the mortal world and seize it for her Court."

"Yes," I said dryly. "She mentioned that while she was threatening all that I love."

"I don't want that," he said. "But don't jump to any conclusions. It's not out of altruism."

"Of course not."

"It would break the game – that's why I don't like it. It would ruin my plans. It would make my ultimate goal impossible."

"And that is ..."

"Not something I'm willing to share."

I snorted.

"And what do I have to do with that."

"I will keep you out of her hands by any trick necessary. I will lie. I will deceive. I will carve my body into pieces and sell it a piece at a time to keep you to myself."

I froze.

He sounded ... crazy.

Worse.

He was never going to let me out of this cage if that was how he felt. I was never going to be free again when he was the only one able to set me free.

"Could we lock the mortal world with that key? The one you stole from me?"

He chuckled.

"I've thought of it."

"If I went to the mortal world with my father, you could lock it behind us and that would be the end of my sister's ambitions."

"And what? You'd leave the children behind?"

I didn't know how to answer that.

"I know you won't," he said. "Giving up isn't in your nature. And it's not in Hulanna's nature, either. She will find another way to open the door between worlds. And now you need to stop yammering. We are nearly to the Bridge. And when we arrive, you must remain silent. I will do whatever I have to do to get you close to your sister's pocket, and you must take that seed while I keep her distracted."

"Agreed," I hissed. Whatever he did, I wouldn't care if he just got me a chance to free my father.

Chapter Twenty-Five

We soared down from the sky and alighted along a sea-bay. A long, suspended bridge crossed the bay with a massive statue on either side. They were shaped like two winged women with their arms held out holding up the bridge – only their dresses were sculpted as torn and shredded and their faces were depicted in horrified screams.

I shuddered at the sight.

"The Bridge doesn't go anywhere," I remarked.

"Don't speak."

"Is it magic?"

"Do you want to do this, or are you backing out? If you want to do this, silence yourself. I may only have one ear, but your sister still possesses both of hers."

The Bridge really didn't lead to anywhere. It just spanned the bay. There were no villages on either side of the bridge. No ports or communities, though out in the brackish gray sea I thought I might see an island. What point was a Bridge that had no purpose? But then again, what point was there in filling your land with colossal and horrific statues?

Why did I expect common sense from the Fae who certainly weren't sensible or common?

I drew my bow from my pack, strapped on my quiver and strung the bow. Whatever came next, it was bound to be trouble.

Scouvrel skirted the bay as the sun began to set, creeping along the coastline until he reached the legs of the great statue. A tunnel was carved through her skirts to the Bridge. He mounted the marble steps and began his ascent. I watched it all from his waist level as my cage bounced and jostled against his legs as he walked. I was getting used to the motion. It still gave me headaches, but the nausea didn't surface anymore.

Where did they find enough marble to carve these statues from? Had it all been mined by golems and then shaped by their stone hands? I pulled my blindfold up, but the statues didn't change. They only seemed to vibrate slightly as if they were alive and frozen in place, rather than made of stone.

I shuddered and pulled it down again.

There were Fae on the Bridge. I recognized Werex and Hulanna and each of them had three others with them, clearly of their courts. But there was no sign of Cavariel and no sign of an encampment or any other retainers. How odd.

"Knave," my sister hissed as we approached.

With a rasp of steel, her retainers drew weapons and so did Werex and his two female orc guards.

"Lady," he said, and I could hear the mocking smirk in his voice.

"You have the cage back," she acknowledged.

"You'll have to bid a lot higher to get it from me once more," Scouvrel said, stepping closer. I stood at the edge of the cage, craning my neck to look up at their faces. We weren't close enough for me to try to pick my sister's pocket, but even so, all I saw were chins and noses. "And I'd prefer bids that don't make me work so hard."

"You mistake the situation, Knave. I let her go. What do I need her for when she can't get out of that cage?" Hulanna asked sweetly.

"Are you saying you don't want her?" Scouvrel asked, a note of danger in his voice. And now I was worried. My value to him lay in my ability to thwart my sister.

"We're busy here," my sister said, shaking her skirts dismissively. "Go peddle your wares somewhere else."

"Oh, Lady of Cups," Scouvrel teased. "Blushing so pink for the Lord of Silk."

She hissed.

"See? Even knaves know things. What good would it be to align yourself with a fallen court? He can't help you – not with half his Court hanging in silken bags on the Cliffs of Decay. They'll die the worst possible deaths, and no one will remember them – and the Lord of Silk put them there. Are you so devastated by your loss of this little trophy that you wish to join them? I've heard that they scream and scream until they cannot scream any longer, slowly dying in their own sweat and tears."

She scoffed. "I don't need her. And I would think you would be the one nursing a loss. Your dignity is half gone. There isn't a female Fae in this land who would want a male with only one ear."

"I grieve the loss even now," he said flippantly. "And yet, I have a better offer for you than cages that can't be opened."

"Then speak it so I may dismiss you."

He stepped closer and I held my breath as her blush pink skirts filled my view. I began to reach and then she stepped back. I pulled my arm back in the cage as fast as I could. My heart was pounding. I didn't dare get caught.

"Oh, don't be so coy, Lady," Scouvrel said. "Surely you'll let me offer a little affection with my offer."

"Cavariel," Hulanna started to protest.

"Is a dog and would expect me to be one, also."

He was trying to kiss her? Of course. I should only be surprised that he hadn't trapped her into it.

"I'm not here for kisses with one-eared males, Knave."

"Then trust me when I say that my words are for your ears alone."

Werex grunted. "You don't trust Twilight, Knave? That's the first reasonable thing you've said here on the Bridge of Reason."

"You know what the Bridge does, Werex," Scouvrel said. "How it makes your intentions freeze within you, twisting to paths you didn't expect. It's why you're meeting the Lord of Silk here. Why not let the Lady treat with me here? Perhaps the luck the Bridge brings will gain her a bargain she doesn't expect."

Werex huffed but Hulanna's voice was crystal clear.

"If you have an offer, make it."

And this time, when Scouvrel stepped in close to whisper in her ear, she didn't back up I leaned out as far as I could from my cage, finding her pocket immediately and plunging my arm inside.

I couldn't hear their whispers above me except for the susurrations of their voices. If I didn't get the seed fast, she might break off the conversation.

I felt something with the tips of my fingers, but my arms were too short.

Frantic, I stuck both arms into the pocket, pulling up the fabric. Gathering it in, like pulling in a net.

I was going to lose my chance. I was going to …

There!

The seed was huge. As big as my head in this cage. I tipped the pocket fabric so that it rolled out onto the rat rug, bouncing off my pack. With a gasp, I leapt toward it, tripping in my haste and sprawling across the floor just in time to grab the seed. Where to hide it? With a gasp, I rolled it under the rug and sat on it. I didn't dare move. If it rolled through the bars, I would lose my father forever.

A slap rang out above my head and then Hulanna was cursing.

"This is no joke, Knave! I should have you skinned alive for suggesting it!"

"Were your blade to grace my skin, you might change your tune," he said, but the skirt was pulling away and the sound of feet repositioning themselves on the bridge made me swallow. What had he said to make her so angry?

"Be gone, filth, or we'll cut you down," Werex growled. "I only hesitate because I have no desire to be Knave in your place."

"I won't apologize," Scouvrel said, backing up as he spoke. "But if you change your mind, you know where I will be."

"I meant what I said," Hulanna said, shaking with fury.

Scouvrel spun and I lost sight of them as he hurried from the bridge.

"You'd better have stolen it," he whispered as he darted between the marble skirts of the screaming statue. "Because I won't be able to go back again unless I fight, and I can't beat Werex."

"I have it," I said. And this time, my heart was pounding with something I hadn't felt in a while ... hope.

Chapter Twenty-Six

"I can't fly by night," he'd said as he snuck through the forest, plunging into it wildly as if he was being chased.

"Do you think they are chasing us?" I asked.

"They'd be fools if they didn't send someone after me. Fools if they didn't suspect something after that madness."

"I need to plant this seed and get my father free."

He clambered up a rocky hill, his breath going ragged. Had I ever heard that ragged sound from him before? It sounded strange coming from Scouvrel who was always perfectly composed even when he was auctioning me off, even when he was imprisoned with an angry unicorn, even when he was sitting on a heap of fae he had slain. Why did I feel so worried for his safety?

"Is he in any condition to travel?" he asked. "I doubt it. If I was torturing him, he'd be little more than a bloody rag by now."

I gaped. I kept forgetting how awful Scouvrel was. His best trick of all was making me trust him despite everything. His best glamor was making me think he wasn't a monster, but every so often his true nature slipped out. He paused, pulling the cage from his belt and setting it on a mossy rock beside him.

"To free your father," he said between panting breaths. "I am going to need to let you out of the cage for a time. I can't pull him off of those spikes. But I don't plan to let you go through the portal. Only him. Which means, it would be best if you freed him there. At the portal. And then you will get back in the cage and we will carry on as we always have."

"And if I won't?" I asked with a trembling voice. Because it sounded like the perfect opportunity to me – the chance to leave this awful place behind. In the back of my mind, I felt shame for that thought. After all, the children would still be here, trapped in this evil world.

"Then your father suffers for all eternity. And that will only increase my reputation as the Knave."

"I don't want that," I admitted.

He had me stuck ... again. Every time I thought there was an opportunity, he sealed it up! He was always a step ahead of me and I didn't know what he wanted. How did you negotiate with someone when you didn't know what they wanted?

"Then we are agreed. We'll free your father when we get to the portal. Try to ease that seed into your pack. It's hard to hear you when you're sitting in the middle of the cage. I want you up by the bars."

"Because I care so much about what you want," I grumbled, but I did ease the seed out from under the rat skin and secured it in my pack.

I had to pull my old clothing out to fit it in. They were dry but wrinkled and smelled of mildew. I sighed as I let them fall through the bars of the cage into the moss below. I was stuck with Scouvrel's feather clothing that matched him like we were a set. Except he was a gloriously beautiful Fae with jet black hair, pointed ears, and a cruel smile and I was a mere mortal of negligible beauty, a cranky attitude, and vulnerable health. We did not match at all.

He trekked through the forest through the deep plum night until we reached a wide clearing around a blossoming plum tree. White and pink blossoms, glowing in my second sight, fluttered down from the tree and drifted in heaps around the bases of the simpler trees. Scouvrel took up a place nearby and began to make a call like an animal – sort of like the call for a deer, but different somehow.

We waited for almost half an hour as he called and listened. Listened and called. I almost thought I heard something responding – a small grunt here, the snap of a twig there. But why was he calling in game? This was no time to hunt.

Out of the trees, a magnificent stag strode and I barely had time to catch my breath. It was smaller than the Sooth's stag had been. Where that had been a giant, this one was the size of a real stag. Its antlers were not like the bucks at home – these ones reached far forward with small paddles on the ends. Cobwebs tangled between them and one of the plum blossoms landed in the cobwebs, sticking there.

Scouvrel called again, raising his hands as it stepped closer. Its pelt was bright white, tinted with patches of light blue like skim milk. I held my breath as it crept closer. I'd never been so near to a living stag of this size. It could turn and trample us in a moment. It huffed a cloud of hot air into the night, turning to a white cloud around it almost instantly. And then, as the beast took another step forward, Scouvrel reached out his hand for its muzzle.

I expected it to spook.

I did not expect it to kneel and let him mount it.

My breath caught in my throat, my eyes widening at the sight. This time, I didn't lift the blindfold. I didn't want to see how the stag really looked – I just wanted to enjoy the beauty of this moment.

Scouvrel held my cage high as he mounted and for the first time in my life, I was being carried by a stag. His antlers obscured my view as he sprang up to all fours and then forward into the trees, stepping lightly over fallen logs and tangles of brush. It was hard not to feel a little thrill. I'd watched a thousand bucks and does from my forest blinds at home. I'd watched them walking alone or with companions. I'd watched them eat and drink. Watched them chase each other, or fight, stomping and throwing their racks up to attack each other.

I'd never ridden one. Never expected to ride one.

It was hard not to be pleased.

We rode in silence for a long time as the night passed. I watched for trails in the woods – signs that animals had passed or fed. There was a lot of life in this strange Fae forest. Some of it I recognized. Some of it was foreign. All of it was from a world that wasn't mine.

The night was cold, and I wrapped myself in the rat hide to keep warm. I tried not to think about where it came from. It was warm and that was all I had the right to want.

We were going to get my father home. The idea filled me with a tangle of longing and relief. Relief at the idea that he would be free. Longing, because I knew I couldn't be – not if I was going to do everything else I needed to do.

"Scouvrel," I tried to say, but he shushed me.

"We must be silent," he whispered, barely louder than a breath.

After that I was silent. I watched the magic of the Faewald, overcome for one by the scent of faerie fruit on the wind, the wildness of the sounds around us in the tangled trees and the beauty of our glorious mount. And for a little while, I dreamed of what it could be like here if all of this was what it seemed and not a tangled mess of power and cruelty.

When, eventually, the sun began to rise, I was exhausted.

So was Scouvrel. He leapt from the stag's back without warning and it stopped, looked around and began to strip twigs from a nearby sapling.

Scouvrel, on the other hand, plunged into the woods to a spot where a prodigious fir tree grew, its branches so low that they formed a tent around it, reaching to the ground. He slipped under the close branches and into the needle-filled space, placed the cage on the forest floor, and wrapped himself around it – not close enough to touch the painful iron, but close enough that he seemed to almost be guarding it.

"Almond?" I offered him once he was settled, holding up one of the nuts he'd thrown at me.

All I heard was snores. He was asleep as soon as his gloriously beautiful head lay down on the needles.

With a sigh, I gnawed at the huge almond and then sat down, shivering in my rat rug. I was still trying to decide what I should do to get warm when I drifted off to sleep.

Chapter Twenty-Seven

When Hulanna and I were ten, my father made us a stones board and taught us to play. But while I quickly grew tired of the game, Hulanna adored it, begging everyone to play with her again and again.

She had the knack of knowing exactly where to put her stones to ruin any strategy I tried. And the more she won, the more she adored playing.

One night, when I was preparing to hunt ghouls with my father, Hulanna said, "You think that you're powerful because you can drive back those spirit carrion eaters, Allie. But what you don't realize is that powerful people are the people who get other people to fight for them, not the ones who do the fighting."

Which was silly, because why would Hulanna ever need someone to fight for her? We would always take care of her.

Chapter Twenty-Eight

I woke to Scouvrel's whisper. "Are you awake Little Night-mare?"

I yawned. "How long was I out?"

"An hour. Possibly more."

"Nngh." An hour had not been long enough.

He laughed low in his throat and I rubbed my eyes. It was hard to see him in the dim light. I could barely make out the profile of his face where it was subtly lit by moonlight through the tree branches.

"I want to make peace with you," he whispered. A tantalizing whisper. A tantalizing thought.

"You do? Why?" Of all the things that came to mind at the thought of Scouvrel, peace was not one of them.

He growled. "Is it not enough that I am offering peace? I have never offered it to anyone else."

"It's an offer?" I asked, warily.

"We could bargain for it if you trust that more."

"What do you want ... exactly."

He chuckled, low and devious. "You're learning, aren't you? Our world is tangling you up, too. You used to offer everything without asking anything in return, but now you bargain. Even days ago, you would have accepted peace free and clear, but not now. Now you want to know the terms."

"So, what," I huffed, sitting up and pulling my braid out. "That just means I'm smart. I'm learning."

"You are." There was regret in his voice. The dark took on a new quality – still velvet and thick, but less dark than before. "Here are my terms: I've already promised you lifelong friendship in our bargain in your world. A promise, I might add, that has chafed a bit. Particularly yesternight when you pitched that fit at me."

"That's not a term," I shot back. In the distance, the sky was moving from black to purple. "And it wasn't a fit. You richly deserved my ire."

He made an annoyed sound at the back of his throat. "I was getting to the terms. If you only had the patience to wait!"

I waited. The sky lightened to soft lilac.

"I want your lifelong friendship. It's only asking for what I've already given you," he said.

"And in exchange?" I asked, tensing. What would he offer me?

"In exchange, I'll make peace with you and I will not interfere in how you go about setting your father free."

I swallowed. That was fair. He'd already said he'd bring me to the portal to release my father, but there hadn't been a true bargain there. Now, I had one.

"Agreed," I whispered. "I vow to be your lifelong friend."

"I vow to let you free your father," he said. He paused and as the light grew to a dull white and his achingly beautiful eyes watched me, he spoke again. "It's good that there is peace between us, Nightmare. I cannot bear your wrath."

I swallowed. He looked like he meant that.

What should I make of that? Was he playing games with my weak mortal mind again ... or was he truly my friend?

"Get some sleep, Scouvrel," I said, masking my emotion with my tone.

He laid back closing his eyes, and I began to hum to him. After all, if I was going to be his friend, I might as well start now. I hummed my favorite lullaby until my eyelids grew heavy and I leaned against my pack with its precious seed and drifted off to sleep again.

I woke to a noonday sun and Scouvrel standing half-naked, inspecting a wound on his side.

"Almost healed," he said with a grin.

Wordlessly, I unwrapped my own bandage to see my hand was almost fully healed.

"This isn't possible," I breathed.

"The Faewald works differently than your world," he said with a shrug. "Ready to fly?"

"This place heals people?"

He shrugged. "Not exactly. It's more that time flows differently here. But you knew that."

I shuddered.

He yanked his lacy white shirt and raven feather coat back over his body, not even bothering to lace them up despite the brisk cold of the morning, scooped up my cage and climbed out from under the tree. I was still surprised every time I saw his wings unfurl. They looked like smoke. They shouldn't have been able to support a songbird.

And yet, we were rising into the air and sailing up above the trees.

"We just need to get over the mountains and then we'll be free and clear." He sounded almost cheerful as he shot up into the sky.

"Does the magic ever wear out?" I asked. "Will your wings fade away and leave us to fall?"

"Not today!" he lifted the cage so I could see the happy grin on his face. He didn't look like he'd slept only a few hours on a floor of needles under a tree.

But I did. Hurriedly, I pulled out my braid, combed through my hair with my fingers and braided my hair again. I took a drink from my water skin, rinsing my mouth and splashed a little on my face.

"Let's go free your father, Nightmare. And then you and I will go put fear into our enemies' hearts and subdue their spirits!"

"I should hum you to sleep every night if this is my reward," I said dryly.

"Indeed, you should, Nightmare." He winked. "Perhaps I will bargain for that next time we bargain together. It seems a worthy prize."

"You can't afford it," I said, but there was no bite to my words. His delight this morning was contagious, and I couldn't help but start to hope that things really might work out.

We were going to free my father and then who knew? Maybe we could convince Hulanna not to be a horrific evil. Maybe I could even free those little children I'd seen. Maybe we could do the impossible together and survive it all. Maybe we could even be friends.

Everything seemed possible on a day like today. I felt my heart and breathing relaxing, my spirits lifting as we soared between stark mountains and past spectacular waterfalls and jagged ridges.

Not all the Faewald was awful. If you stayed to the unpopulated places, it was rather beautiful. I'd grown so used to my second sight that I hardly knew anything else. I could stay here long enough to right wrongs. I might even like Scouvrel's company if he stayed in this good mood.

We stopped at one of the waterfalls for Socuvrel to drink and for me to refill my thimble and wash out the other one. We ate the dried fruit and nuts and the first bleeding edge of sunset was upon us when we leapt again into the skies. Scouvrel's laugh was clear as crystal and his eyes sparkled and danced in the last rays of the sun.

"Truth or Lie?" he asked.

"Are we playing that old game again?"

"We never stopped. Truth or Lie? We can be friends."

"Truth," I said. And I even meant it.

It made me feel warm inside, like I could carry my own private fire inside my chest.

He was still smiling as he dove down toward the smoke waterfall beneath us. Still smiling as we landed on the mossy ground near the ring of rocks where we had first entered the world. Still smiling as I dug the seed out of my bag and threw it to the ground.

But when the tree rose up and grew in place and my tortured father was forced from its core still nailed to the tree, neither of us was smiling anymore.

Chapter Twenty-Nine

"You fools!" Cavariel sprang out from the bole of the still-growing tree. His eyes glowed with the delight of surprising us before they shifted to dark malevolence.

I gasped, reaching for my bow – for all the good it would do in this moment. I pulled it out, stringing it in one fluid motion and strapping on my arrows. I pulled one of the arrows out and nocked it, ready.

Cavariel drew a sword, too – a flashy thing with a gold crossguard and cabochon rubies. He held it in a relaxed grip, but that worried me. Only a truly great swordsman could be that relaxed, right?

Scouvrel drew his pin from a rapier scabbard. He hadn't replaced that yet? He whipped it through the air, making a ripping sound as he flourished it – more like he was drawing a sword for a performance than for a fight. I would have snorted in derision, except that I'd seen him slaughter two Fae with that thing.

"What is this, Cups?" he asked, arching a single eyebrow in a question.

I heard my father moan and something inside me went cold as ice. Cavariel was here to stop us from freeing him. I couldn't allow that.

"A clever little trap for some clever little prey," Cavariel said. He tossed his sword from one hand to the other, letting it spin twice in the distance between hands. Was he serious? Did

Fae think that coy lines delivered in intimidating tones and little flourishes were an actual substitute for the part where you stabbed someone?

"I can best you with a blade and be done in time to savor tea with my choice of ladies," Scouvrel said coolly, slicing the air with his pin as if testing its balance. I tried not to bounce too much on my toes. I couldn't get out of the cage any faster than Scouvrel let me.

But yes, it did seem that coy comments and dramatics were going to be their weapons of choice.

"Don't think I came with only a sword in my hand, Knave. I brought the Balance," Cavariel said.

There was a cracking sound from above us and then the two-faced, two-winged Balance stepped out of the bark of the tree and drifted down, a scroll in one hand and a pen in the other. Scouvrel froze and I searched his face as his eyes sped from one of the newcomers to the other and then back.

"Better if you'd brought the Kinslayer," he said, but he sounded shaken.

"There are only moments left to bid. You did say seven days, correct?" Cavariel said. "And my dear wife has placed a bid with the Balance."

"It can't be higher than what I'll bid," Scouvrel said.

Cavariel smirked. "Really? This caged mortal means so much to you? Perhaps you should reconsider your priorities. Cups has no argument with you – not now. You are free to go back to your role in the Courts. We have our own matters to deal with – our own campaigns to battle, our own grudges to repay."

My father moaned from behind them and my heart squeezed. This couldn't be happening. My sister had stolen me. How could she have placed a bid and also realized that I would steal the seed from her? She was two steps ahead of me. Again.

Scouvrel tensed, the end of his sword wavering slightly as if he was moments from plunging it toward Cavariel.

"Long I've tolerated you and your Court, Lord of Cups," he said in a low tone. "Don't think that I don't remember how you trapped me previously and thought to end me in the mortal realm as a scout for you and your lady. You have been no friend to me and no friend to my former Court. There will be no peace between you and me as long as blood runs in my veins."

He froze in place when the Balance stepped forward, one hand raised to calm him, the pen still clutched in it.

"Peace, Knave, until this matter is settled. Spilled blood won't change the bids. The Lady of Cups has bid six months of her husband's life in servitude to the Balance in exchange for the prisoner." He looked apologetically to Scouvrel. "You did not set out who would be paid the price, Knave, only that the highest bid of any kind would win. You've been bested. Accept it with grace or defy the Law of Games."

I couldn't see Scouvrel's face. I wanted to see it. What was he thinking? Had he not planned for this? He planned for everything.

"So, she just bid someone else's service?" I said, my voice climbing higher and higher in my nervousness. "She can do that? What if I bid *my* husband's service for a year? Would that mean I could buy my own freedom?"

"Do you place such a bid?" the Balance asked, raising an eyebrow, pen poised to write. "You have time left to make it, if you do."

"You don't have a husband," Cavariel objected at the same time that Scouvrel said, "No."

I laughed sarcastically. "Sure. I bid my husband's servitude to the Balance for one year. There. Does that buy my freedom? Your games are ridiculous."

The cage was shaking as if Scouvrel's hand was shaking. Was it an earthquake? I clutched the bars in my hands. But the Balance and Cavariel seemed to be steady and unmoved.

"No bid from you, Knave of Courts?" the Balance asked coldly.

Scouvrel lifted the cage so I could see his face. I froze at his expression of fury mixed with despair.

"I had planned to give my life for you," he whispered. The cage shook with his rage. "How could I have known that you would offer it first?"

"But – " My words cut off as I looked at our audience – the smug look on the Balance's face. The shock on Cavariel's. My voice came out barely louder than a squeak. "But I'm not married. I have no husband."

The Balance laughed. "Has no one told you, mortal, that the Fae do not make proposals of marriage. We make tricks of marriage. You are married without knowing it. Bidding is closed. The winning bid is the mortal's. All present are bound by my decision on pain of the Death of Silk."

Cavariel began to speak, but his words cut off immediately, his hand only half-raised in the air. Both he and the Balance were frozen – and so was the wind, the trees, everything.

Scouvrel reached into his pocket. His face looked haunted as he drew out the golden key and shoved it at me, setting the cage on the ground so I could only see his black feathered boots.

"Here. It's what you bought. You only have minutes to snatch your father and flee this place. That's all the time I can buy you. Hurry."

I grabbed my pack, held the key to the lock and willed it to open. It opened with a snick and I stepped out, snatching up the cage and slinging it onto my belt, the key going straight into my pocket.

I dashed to my father. He coughed up blood, his head lolling painfully on his chest. With all my might I grabbed the iron nail in his right shoulder, braced a foot against the tree, and pulled with both hands. It wouldn't budge.

"Here," Scouvrel said, shoving me aside.

"You'll burn yourself!"

He growled unintelligibly at me and grabbed the stake anyway, ripping it out of the tree. He dropped it like it was hot. His hands were blazing red, the palms burned by the iron.

"No!" I objected but he was already gripping the other stake. I hurried to grab my father's free arm, draping it over my shoulder.

Scouvrel yanked the second nail out, cursing as he did it. It fell to the moss at our feet and the Fae threw himself under my father's other shoulder just as I was faltering under the weight.

He looked across my father's bowed head at me, fury and loss ripping across his face.

"I had a plan. It was a good plan, and you ruined it," he accused me.

"You married me without telling me!" I shot back, horri-fied.

He grinned through his fury. "Best decision I ever made."

We stumbled together toward the stone circle and I felt a tiny movement in the air around me.

"My magic is fading. Here." He ripped a hair from his head and held it to me. "To power your key."

I took the hair from his burned fingers – they looked bad – fumbling in my pocket for the key and winding the hair around it. Why was my vision so blurry? I wasn't crying, was I?

I looked back at him in horror.

Was I ... did I care about Scouvrel? His evil grin grew wider and I felt my mouth drop open. I cared about his year of servitude. I cared about ruining his plans. When had I started to care?

He leaned across my father, taking advantage of my parted lips and kissed me and for someone so evil, the kiss was surprisingly sweet.

"I respect your ability to fall into traps like a concussed rabbit," he said with a wink.

I grabbed his hand and pulled it up to my lips so that I could kiss the burn.

The look on his face was beyond price. I'd never seen him so shocked.

"I respect your ability to give so generously even when you pretend you don't care."

He smiled, regretfully.

And then he pushed me through the portal.

I gasped. I would have screamed, but it was all I could do to hold onto my father as the Faewald narrowed to a pinprick and then disappeared with a *pop*.

He was gone.

And all I wanted right now was to have him back.

Chapter Thirty

I tumbled out onto the turf of my homeland, my bleeding father clutched in one arm and my heart aching in a way that I couldn't understand. We fell together into the knee-high grass as the smell of the high plains washed over me like a memory of a time passed. Hot tears ran down my cheeks as I clutched at my father.

"Dad?" I whispered, "Can you hear me?"

There was a cry of surprise nearby and I looked up to see who it was. Oh yeah. My vision here was blurry and difficult. There were people nearby and trails of rabbits and other animals. But everything was dark and ghostlike as I looked with my second sight. I was back in the mortal world. That should have made me feel better. But instead, it only made me feel hollow.

I yanked my blindfold up and the world swam into focus.

In front of me, a horse reared. Behind it, about a dozen other horses stomped or stepped to the side, spooked – it would seem – by my sudden appearance.

"Allie Hunter?" I would have recognized that voice anywhere. "Is that you?"

I scrambled to my feet, unable to pull my father up with me.

Heldra surged forward with her voice – only this wasn't Heldra … was it? She was just as beautiful as I remembered. But her long hair was pulled up in a knot and her figure had filled out completely, her face growing more *her* somehow. Deeper. Lined a bit. Just – more. She looked like her mother.

She was older, I realized. And the child clutching her skirts looked just like her. A girl of about two years.

Time is different here.

Was it ever.

A creeping chill washed over me like a bucket of ice water had been thrown over my head.

I looked up at the man on the horse. The one holding a mandolin in one hand and clutching the pommel of a sword with his other hand. Olen looked about ten years older than he had been when I last saw him. He sat his horse tall and proud, not stooping any longer. And he was wearing livery of some kind. Behind him, all the other dozen horsemen wore livery, too.

I gasped.

My eyes darted from his face – fuller, like Heldra's. More lived in. Mature. To hers again and then back. And I felt a pain to my heart like a dagger.

The little boy. The child I'd seen.

There was no doubt now in my mind that the child was Olen's.

"You have a son," I said without thinking.

"Where is he?" Heldra sounded panicked. "We lost Petyr only two days ago! We don't know where he is! Did you see him in that cursed land?"

"Yes," I gasped.

Olen's face crumpled and he tried to charge his horse through the circle but all that did was make the horse run across the grass to the other side. His curses echoed across the valley.

Heldra's expression pinched in the corners. I wanted to gather her into my arms.

I had the key to the portal. I spun, holding it out, but nothing happened. I'd already used Scouvrel's hair on it. And it wouldn't work for me a second time without some magic to fuel it.

I felt numb as I leaned over my father, turning him so that I could wipe his face with the hem of my shirt.

"Water," he mumbled, and I dug the waterskin from my pack, gently dribbling some between his chapped, bleeding lips.

My tears were flowing hot and fast now. Hot and fast for my father and his wounds. Hot and fast for Olen and Heldra and their lost son Petyr. Hot and fast for the strange loss I felt at the thought of Scouvrel pushing me through the portal. I wiped them awkwardly with the back of my hand.

"Can you help me?" I asked, my voice strangled. "My father needs help. Can any of you help us?"

I tried to feed my pain into my internal fire. But there was nothing there to feed. My fire had gone out.

My sister had been so much smarter than I was. Even in defeating her, I had lost.

The next hours passed in a blur. My shock at the changes in the town was reflected in the shock of every townsperson who saw me – the girl missing for ten years who looked exactly the same.

They'd made Skundton an outpost now, claimed by Queen Anabetha. Olen Chanter was her Knight here, the other men of the town served in rotation as his militia. It was hard to square this tough, fighting Olen with the boy I'd known. Even when he put a heavy hand on my shoulder and promised we would have revenge on the Fae.

It was hard to see the town – triple the size it had been when I left it and boasting a stable for horses now and two inns.

It was even harder when they brought me to my mother – living with Olen's parents in their little house. Olen's father sat on a rocking chair and never looked up as we approached. He whistled constantly to himself, sad, longing tunes.

"We can't make him stop. He hums even in his sleep," Olen said sadly. "It has been that way for ten years, since we found him beside the portal. I'd gone up there to look for you."

Only a seven-day ago for me. Ten years for him.

My mother's gasp when we came through the door, the way her knees buckled, the extra gray in her hair and lines around her eyes – each one was a knife to my heart. But her hug was like healing balm.

"Allie, oh my Allie!" she'd said through her sobs.

Even that was nothing compared to the heartbreaking hope on her face when we carried my father in on a litter. She was busy with him now, stitching and binding his wounds, washing his body tenderly in the way of a woman whose dead had returned.

And I sat before the Chanter's fire with Olen's mother. And I opened the book my ancestors had written.

"Do you have ink?" I asked her. "And a pen?"

And when she brought them, I began to write. Not in vague hints or rhyming prophecy. I wrote clear and black and as fully as I could remember. I wrote everything from beginning to end.

Tomorrow, there might be no one else to tell this story and ready my people for the next time they needed it. Tomorrow there might be no one to warn of tricks of marriage or deceptions and bargains. There might be no one left to warn of the coming Feast of Ravens.

Because tomorrow I would go back to the circle. I was going to dance around it and call the Fae. And this time when they came, I would be ready.

Read more of Allie Hunter's story in Fae Nightmare: Book Three of the Twisted Fae series.

If you enjoyed Fae Hunter, please consider leaving a review[1].

Reviews help fellow readers know what books to read and they help me know to prioritize my time and energy to that series. Thank you in advance!

---

1. https://www.amazon.com/review/create-review?asin=B07XLPZTFR

Behind the Scenes:

USA Today bestselling author, Sarah K. L. Wilson loves spinning a yarn and if it paints a magical new world, twists something old into something reborn, or makes your heart pound with excitement ... all the better! Sarah hails from the rocky Canadian Shield in Northern Ontario – learning patience and tenacity from the long months of icy cold – where she lives with her husband and two small boys. You might find her building fires in her woodstove and wishing she had a dragon handy to light them for her

Sarah would like to thank **Julie Thomas** and **Eugenia Kollia** for their incredible work in beta reading and proofreading this book. Without their big hearts and passion for stories, this book would not be the same.

Sarah has the deepest regard for the talent of her phenomenal artist Luciano Fleitas who created the gorgeous cover art that accompanies this book. Without his work, it would be so much harder to show off this story the way it deserves!

Thanks also to the Noble Order of Female Fantasy Authors who keep me sane – sort of. And for my beloved husband, Cale and sons Neville and Leif who are endlessly patient as I talk to them about bookish passions.

www.sarahklwilson.com[1]

Follow Sarah to keep up with fun updates:

INSTAGRAM[2]

---

1.   https://www.sarahklwilson.com/bridge-of-legends

[FACEBOOK](3)
[AMAZON](4)
[NEWSLETTER](5)

2. https://www.instagram.com/sarahklwilson

3. http://www.facebook.com/sarahklwilson

4. https://www.amazon.com/-/e/B0064MSJRE

5. https://www.subscribepage.com/brandawareness